DU

MW01096495

Adventures in the Liaden Unive

Sharon Lee and Steve Miller

COPYRIGHT PAGE

DUE DILIGENCE

Adventures in the Liaden Universe® Number 24

Pinbeam Books

www.pinbeambooks.com

This is a work of fiction. All the characters and events portrayed in this novel are fiction or are used fictitiously

"Due Diligence" is original to this chapbook

Cover created by Sharon Lee

ISBN: 978-0-9966346-5-6

Due Diligence

I

"For attachment to a criminal endeavor designed to disrupt the operations of this port, evidenced by signed papers recovered, Fer Gun pen'Uldra is fined two cantra, to be assessed from future earnings. Should there be no such earnings within one Standard Year, the amount will be deducted from Fer Gun pen'Uldra's accrued Guild dues, and his name shall be struck from the rolls."

That was steep, that was, Fer Gun thought, his belly tight and his breath coming short and shallow. Two cantra? Still, he was a Jump pilot–a damned good Jump pilot, as he needn't say himself, since the record supported him–he might be able to find a berth–

"In addition," Solcintra Pilots Guild Master continued, "Fer Gun pen'Uldra's license to pilot is suspended for one Standard year. After such time, he shall be eligible for reinstatement when a pilot in good standing testifies on behalf of Fer Gun pen'Uldra before the Guild, and guarantees his good behavior as a pilot for the following Standard Year."

It was as if a fist had slammed into his belly. For a moment, he couldn't see; couldn't breathe. They were taking his license! He was–a two cantra fine, and his license suspended? How–

"Fer Gun pen'Uldra," said the Guild Master. "Do you have anything further to say?"

Say? What could he say? That it hadn't been his signature on the damned paper? Of course, it had been his signature. That he hadn't any notion what his cousin Jai Kob had in mind to do on–or to–Solcintra Port? That he was a pilot, that was all and everything he'd ever wanted to be. His cousins did their business; his business was to fly them where business called.

He managed a breath.

"No, sir." His voice was firm, if subdued. "Nothing further to say."

The Guild Master looked to the Port Proctor standing at the corner of the table. The Proctor stepped to Fer Gun's side, her face impassive.

"Fer Gun pen'Uldra, relinquish your license to the Pilots Guild. When the terms are met, it will be returned to you."

There was black at the edges of his vision. His license. Turn over his license to this blank-faced flunky? He would die before he did anything so daft! For a moment, indeed, he thought he would turn over his fist and make a run–

But that was no good, he told himself. The Guild would blacklist the license, then, and he'd be in worse case than he stood right now.

So.

"It's in the jacket," he told the Proctor and his voice was nowhere near steady, now. "Inside right breast pocket."

"Understood," she answered, and watched while he slid his hand inside his jacket, and fingered the card–his license to fly–out of the hidden pocket, and offered it to her between two fingers.

She received it without comment, and returned to her place at the corner of the table.

The Guild Master inclined his head.

"Fer Gun pen'Uldra, you may go."

#

Well, and he'd gone–of course he had. An overnight in the holding cell had been plenty enough for him. It might fairly be said that having no place to go was a superior situation.

Out on the Port, he paused to get his bearings, acutely aware of the absence of his flight card. Not that it had weighed so much, but knowing it was gone created an imbalance in the fit of his jacket.

He took a breath, then another, ignoring the rumbling in his stomach. They hadn't fed him in the holding cell. They might have done, if he had asked, but it hadn't occurred to him to ask them for anything.

What he wanted now was *Lady Graz*, though Jai Kob's welcome for a wingless pilot was not likely to be warm. His value had been in his license. Remove that single value and he was only the dim-witted singleton, dependent on Telrune's charity. It was entirely possible that his cousins would leave him here, once they found his situation.

Fer Gun squared his shoulders.

Well, then. They need not *know* his situation. It was his business, wasn't it? Oh, he would definitely cite the two-cantra fine at Jai Kob, so he would! But the loss of his ticket...

It came to him that his skill had not been taken from him. He was still a pilot, and a damned good one, wherever his license reposed. Granted, he could not record his flight-time, and he would therefore not advance in the Guild.

But, he could still pilot a spaceship.

Jai Kob need not know that Fer Gun had lost his license.

He had his bearings, now, and turned east, toward the edge-yard where they'd brought the *Lady* down, and locked her. His stomach complained as he moved into a quick walk. He ignored it.

#

"Oh," said the dockman wisely, when Fer Gun arrived at the office, to find the board listing only three ships. "You've come about the quick-hire, have you? You're only a half-day too late. They meant *quick*, they did, and they weren't particular, either. Took the first good card that walked in the door."

Fer Gun stared at him.

"*Lady Graz*," he said slowly, to be certain he understood; "she's lifted?"

"That's right," the dockman said. "Regular pilot walked out soon as they hit port. Found a better opportunity, I'll wager. That knife cuts both ways, though, on Solcintra. The owners didn't have any trouble at all, hiring new."

"Thank you," Fer Gun said, feeling the absence of his license like a blade through his heart. He took a breath.

"Is there somewhere nearby where I might. . .buy a beer?"

#

Teetering on the edge of the Low Port, the bar was called *Wingman's Folly*, and the beer was cheap for a reason. The few coins in his pocket might even, Fer Gun thought, stretch to a bowl of soup, though if the food were equal to the quality of the beer. . .

Wingless and broke, near enough; and Jai Kob had set it up; had deliberately schemed to remove the idiot cousin.

And that, Fer Gun told himself, taking a cautious sip of his so-called beer, was what came of asking questions. They had not been deep questions; they had not been questions inappropriate to a pilot, though they had touched–lightly!–on the business Jai Kob conducted, with Cousin Vin Dyr's able assistance.

Two questions, and he had rendered himself a liability, abandoned to the mercies of the Port Proctors and the Guild, without money, without kin, without contacts, his only means of making a living residing by now in a safe at Guild Headquarters...

Jai Kob might not have known that they would take his license, Fer Gun told himself. And, in truth, Jai Kob's knowledge of the universe was not in his queue of immediate worries. Those included finding some sort of food, a bed, and work.

Work ought to be possible, he told himself, nursing his beer. He was strong; he had a good head for numbers. He could take orders–gods, couldn't he just! In any wise, he *could* work, and he would work. The important thing was not to slip over the line from Mid-Port to Low. He was accounted good in a fight, but he had no illusions regarding the odds of near-term survival on Low Port for a single, partnerless pilot, wearing spaceleather and a good pair of boots.

The thing then was to go right when he left the *Wingman*–up to Mid-Port, Low Port at his back. He'd ask at the docks and the warehouses, first. Long-term would be good, but day-labor would do. The first priorities were to feed himself, and find that bed...

"More beer, Pilot?"

The barkeep was young and pretty, and it passed through Fer Gun's mind that he might, if he were clever, flirt his way into a bed for a night–or even several.

The idea hung there for a moment, before he rejected it. What could a lad–even a pretty lad who doubtless commanded pretty tips?–earn in such a place, situated as it was? Enough to feed and shelter himself, *and* a hungry pilot, too?

"No more beer, I thank you," he said, putting more of his coins than he ought on the bar.

"Come again, pilot," the 'keeper said, and swept away to tend the other custom

Fer Gun off his stool, and headed for the door, standing back as it swung open, then stepping forward.

"Going so soon?" A woman's voice very nearly in his ear. "I thought you might share a glass with me."

The mode was Comrade, the voice unfamiliar. As was the face, when he turned to look at her.

The first thing he noticed was her height–taller than he was, which wasn't usual. She wore a Jump pilot's jacket, scarred and soft with wear. Her hair was blonde, pulled back into a knot at her nape; her face sharp; her eyes blue. Not a beauty, though she could pass. There was something about her drew and held the eye. She was also, he saw on third look, older than he was. Considerably so.

"Pilot," he said, giving her Comrade, because were not all pilots comrades? "Pilot, I do not know you."

"And I do not know you!" she said with a broad grin. "That is why we ought to drink a glass together, and perhaps share a small meal. They put together a very edible cheese plate here, for which I vouch."

He hesitated, which was pure madness. If the blonde pilot had a fancy for a younger bedmate, then she was the answer to tonight's problem, at least.

And if she were a thief, or part of a wolf pack, she would, he thought with a certain amount of irony, shortly be very disappointed in him.

So.

"Thank you," he said, inclining his head.

"Excellent–here!" She guided him to a table well-back from the door, and Fer Gun marked how those at the bar kept their backs to the room, while those at table did not look up. "Sit–sit!" said his new comrade. "I will order."

She threw a hand in the air. The pretty 'tender looked up as if he had heard the gesture, ducked out from behind the bar, and walking briskly toward their table.

"Service, Pilot?" he asked.

She smiled at him, and bespoke a bottle, two glasses and a "nuncheon plate," to share between comrades.

The boy bowed, and left them, whereupon the blonde pilot flowed bonelessly into the chair across from him and folded her hands on the tabletop.

"My name is Chi," she said, with an informality that might yet equally come from a pilot shopping a bedmate, or a wolf casing a mark.

"My name is Fer Gun," he answered, matching her tone.

"In fact your name is Fer Gun pen'Uldra," she said calmly. "I have a proposition to put before you."

"No!" he snapped, shoving the chair back–and freezing on the way to his feet, staring down at her hand on his wrist.

"Will you not even hear it?" she asked.

Her grip was firm, but not painful. It was, in fact, very nearly a comrade's touch. He raised his eyes to meet hers, finding a sort of amused kindness in her face.

"I will not go grey–or dark," he growled.

"All honor to you," she said lightly. "My proposal is nothing to tarnish your *melant'i*."

She paused, brows contracting somewhat.

"There are those who might argue the point, but I think they need not concern us."

"Let me go," he said, though he could have easily broken her grip.

She did so on the instant, and inclined her head.

"Forgive me."

He took a breath, thinking he would rise and leave her, after all–but here came the 'tender, bearing a full tray. The plate came down between them; the bottle went to the fair-haired pilot, and the glasses, too.

Fer Gun's stomach loudly reminded him of the recent abuses visited upon it–and was it not balance, to eat the pilot's food and drink her wine, while he listened to her proposal?

"Thank you," she said to 'tender, and poured the wine, offering Fer Gun the first glass.

He waited until she had poured her own, inclined his head and sipped, finding the wine far superior to the beer. Apparently, Pilot Chi had deep pockets, which would account for her thinking she might order all to her liking.

"Eat," she said, and reached to the plate herself.

He did the same, and at his stomach's prompting twice more before he recalled that he was in company, and folded his arms on the tabletop.

"In its simplest form," Pilot Chi murmured, "my proposition is this: I require a child."

Fer Gun did not choke, but it was a near thing. He studied his comrade's arresting face, and found no hint of mockery, or madness, only a clear-eyed earnestness.

"Why not go to Festival?" he asked.

"A reasonable question. I seek to avoid notoriety. . ."

She paused, and again there was that quizzical, and slightly self-mocking expression.

"*Additional* notoriety. And, sadly, Festival-get will not answer my purpose, though it would seem, as you say, the simplest solution. The child must arrive properly by contract, above reproach and unexceptional in the eyes of the world. Also, I fear that I require a pilot to stand father, and I see from your records that you are a very fine pilot, indeed."

He blinked.

"My records? How did you see my records?"

"Ah. I have access to the Guild files."

He took a breath.

"That must be expensive," he said, trying to match her tone of calm nonchalance.

"Not at all."

She plucked a tidbit from the tray, and popped it into her mouth.

Fer Gun took a breath.

"If you've seen my records, you have seen that I am convicted of crimes against the port, and have had my wings clipped for it. I may fly again when I produce two cantra to pay my fine, and also a witness to my reformed character."

"Yes. Your cousins are very clever, are they not?"

He considered her.

"If you're looking for brains in addition to reactions, you'll want to shop elsewhere."

"No, I do not allow you to be stupid, merely naive. Naivety may be mended."

A sip of wine, and a glint of blue eyes. Fer Gun ate another bit of cheese, and a round of bread, washed down with a careful sip of wine.

Putting his glass aside, he leaned toward Pilot Chi.

"Clan Telrune is outworld, and Low House. We're scoundrels, in a word, and, so I learn, there is not even honor among kinsmen."

"If it comes to that, my own clan not infrequently throws out rogues. We do better by our kin than Telrune would seem to do, but, then, we are much poorer in cousins. I do not wish to rush you, pilot, but may I know if you find my proposal of any interest?"

He sipped his wine, considering.

In well-ordered clans, as even he knew, he would at this juncture place the matter in the hands of his delm. As Telrune was nothing like well-ordered, and there being no gain to the clan in breeding him, the last pen'Uldra, he supposed he might make his own decision in the case. After all, the proposed child would remain with Pilot Chi, and burden Telrune not at all. Unlike himself, who was, as Aunt Jezmin often said, nothing more than another mouth to feed, useless as all his Line had been, and luck he'd been born able to least to think with his fingers, since his brain was only a hindrance to him.

There might, perhaps, be something in the business for Telrune, should Pilot Chi prove to be of a clan useful to the delm's on-going schemes. But the truth was that Telrune's focus *was* scheming. He had never, in Fer Gun's memory, negotiated a contract for alliance–or for any other thing. Mostly, his kin allied as suited themselves; babies were born, and came into the House haphazard, though Telrune did, often, remember to record their names.

In the case of the proposal before him. . .he found himself largely neutral. The issue would be no concern of his. And if it came to the pilot herself, his proposed contract-wife, she looked likely to give good sport in bed. There was that tendency to order all to her own satisfaction, but he was accustomed to have someone else do his thinking for him, now wasn't he?

And among orderly Houses, he thought, his wine glass arrested on its way to his lips, as he suddenly recalled a custom he had never truly learned. . . In proper Clans, contract-spouses were given a pay-out, once the conditions of the contract were met. It might be that Pilot Chi represented the manner in which he might pay his fine. Also, it would fall to Pilot Chi's clan to feed him, and clothe him, and shelter him during the term of the contract. In that free year, then, he might order his affairs, make contacts, find work. . .

"I am prepared," Pilot Chi said quietly, "to be generous."

He stared at her.

"To Telrune?"

That drew a smile.

"To yourself, though of course Telrune must be accommodated in such a way that the contract does not reflect badly upon the child."

"That's an extra-size lot of respectability you're wanting," he pointed out. "I *did say* we're scoundrels."

"You did. But I've no objection to scoundrels, being one myself. What I *must* have is the seeming of propriety. We will do the thing properly, for the sake of the child, who must be able to deal from a solid foundation."

She picked up the bottle and refreshed their glasses.

"What do you think, Pilot?"

He sipped his wine, and *did* think, for a wonder and a novelty, before meeting her eyes once more.

"I think," he said slowly, "that I will need to know who you are, Pilot. You have the key to my life, but I know nothing of you."

"Fairly said."

She seemed to square her shoulders under the worn leather, and met his eyes firmly.

"I am Chi yos'Phelium Clan Korval."

The floor bucked, and he nearly lost his glass.

Korval.

Everything was illuminated by her name: access to the Guild database, her need of a pilot-father; the necessity of proper adherence to the forms.

"Surely," he managed, his voice breathless in his own ears, "you can do better. Pilot."

She laughed at that and held her hand out to him.

"Do you know? I think that you and I will get on extremely."

He looked from her face to that hand, slim and strong. She was a clever woman; she was older and more experienced than he; it was, he reminded himself, an opportunity.

"I think so, too," he said. And met her hand.

II

Petrella yos'Galan came to the end of the file, flipped to the photo, sighed, and spun the chair so that she faced her twin, leaning with arms crossed against the corner of the desk.

"Well," she said, "he's not in the common way."

Chi half-laughed.

"No, he's barely tamed; and now that he's learnt to distrust kin, he's well on the way to ruination." She tipped her head.

"Wine?"

"Of your kindness."

Chi straightened out of her lean, and crossed the room. Petrella looked once more at the flat-pic on her screen.

A young man, rangy and rough, with unruly dark hair tangled 'round a fierce, bony face. The eyes alone would slay dozens, black as space and hard as obsidian.

Yet, among all this ferocity, there was a hint of sweetness 'round the mouth; a barely perceptible softness in the jutting chin. Not ruined yet, she thought, but wary as a cat, and dangerous.

Chi was of course fully capable, but it had never been her habit to bed dangerously.

A breath of air alerted her, and she moved her eyes from the screen to her sister's face, and received the wine from her hand.

Silently, they lifted their glasses, and drank in unison. Chi sighed.

"His piloting record –" she began. . .

"Is astonishing," Petrella finished. They were identical twins from a clan which had given many to the *dramliz* over the generations. Often, they did not even need to speak aloud. More often, they finished each other's thoughts seamlessly.

"But is it enough?" Chi asked the question Petrella had not.

She leaned over and touched the screen, calling up the boy's record.

"Won a scholarship to Anlingdin, despite the deplorable condition of his House," she murmured. "Graduated early from an accelerated course; 'prenticed on a Looper for the long-side, and mastered Jump before he came twenty-four."

"Whereupon his delm called him home, and his troubles began." Petrella sighed this time. "You *might* have found someone more convenable, you know."

"And young Fer Gun?"

Petrella hesitated.

"Mistress Toonapple often has need of pilots, and she is, so we hear, accounted a fair Boss."

Chi raised her eyebrows.

"Are you advising me to place a pilot into Juntavas hands, sister?" she asked.

Petrella felt a twinge of shame before her twin shook her head.

"Even if that is your advice, it won't answer. The child himself tells me that he will not fly grey–and never dark."

"*Does* he?"

Petrella tipped her head.

"That is. . .promising," she murmured.

"You might say it," Chi agreed, and half-raised her glass.

"There's more, if you'll have it."

"I must," Petrella assure her, "have everything."

"Yes, well. His cousins set him up beautifully, with that contract in hand, and his signature there for all to see. He must have become inconvenient for them, do you think? Perhaps he began asking questions. Jai Kob cho'Fadria–the elder cousin–is something more than a mere scoundrel; the other cousin–Vin Dyr–killed a man in a bar brawl on an outworld, and the proctors bought off."

"So the cousins wanted young Fer Gun out of the way," Petrella said, and raised her eyes to meet Chi's gaze. "Or dead."

"We can do better than either for him, I think," her sister said, and raised her glass.

"As for finding someone more convenable. . ." she continued. . . "the sole Line on the homeworld which always produces a pilot is yos'Galan, and we have crossed lines too recently for that match, even if Sae Zar was willing."

Petrella snorted.

"The mother's twin bedding the halfling nephew. Yes, propriety would be satisfied by that."

"It does become problematical. Young Fer Gun, on the other hand, will offend no one."

"He will offend *every*one," Petrella corrected.

She sipped her wine, thoughtfully.

"Which comes to the same thing, I suppose."

Chi lifted her glass in ironic salute.

Petrella reached to the screen and tapped up Pilot pen'Uldra's picture once more.

"The Code teaches us," she said slowly, her eyes on that space-cold gaze; "that a contract ought benefit both parties. What benefit comes to this boy by making contract with Korval? You will of course stand hostage to his wings, which for him will count for much. But, I wonder, is that enough? He is unpolished. He is, forgive me, not merely Low House, but, as he himself said to you, affiliated with a House composed entirely of rogues and petty thieves. To raise him up, even just for the length of the contract, into the brangle and spite the High Houses. . .He may survive it–he looks a hardy lad–but he will not thrive. He will make errors, possibly errors that will follow him for the rest of his life, and even if not–"

She paused, considering the tattered remnants of sweetness in the hard young face.

"Even if not," she finished, as Chi was silent; "he will mind it, and it will cost him."

She glanced up into her sister's grave eyes.

"It will cost him," she repeated.

Chi inclined her head.

"I agree," she said, her voice as grave as her eyes. "The child cannot thrive in alt, and I will not ask it of him. I intend due diligence, and a careful Balance."

She sipped her wine.

"We may easily, I think, manage the signing, and an afternoon meal."

Petrella frowned slightly.

"Guests chosen from allies and aspirants," she said slowly. "A luncheon, rather than a dinner. Bold he may be, but we do not wish to try his mettle at a full formal affair."

"Precisely. I have it in mind to place him in Ilthiria's hands–though, perhaps her brother would answer better. . ."

"A collaboration might serve best of all," Petrilla said, tipping her head slightly. "Give him enough polish and manner to manage the necessaries–if he's a clever boy and keeps modestly quiet. . .Stay! Allow him to be overawed by his good fortune, and sweetly shy. That should play well."

"My thoughts, yes. So, that Jump is made."

"But what then?" demanded Petrella. "Will you keep the child locked in his rooms? He's a pilot, and very nearly feral. He won't care to be confined."

"Certainly he would not! No, I have in mind to take him off-planet. Korval can afford to be generous. *I* can afford to be generous. How then a business arrangement, negotiated separately from the marriage contract, in which he becomes provisional captain of that small-trader we had been discussing last week? We shall do a tour, and I will introduce him to those who will be useful to him, returning to Liad in time to appease propriety in the matter of the child's arrival. After, the pilot will be released to his rightful business. We might easily steer likely crew, and a trader, in his direction."

She paused, frowning.

"I suppose I will need to retain a share. Small enough not to encumber him; large enough to deter any plans his House might nurture to wrest the enterprise away from the child and repurpose it for their own use."

She moved her shoulders.

"dea'Gauss will contrive."

Petrella sipped her wine, inspecting the thing from all sides. Finally, she put her glass on the desk with a decisive click.

"It will answer. Especially as I have already made arrangements to keep to Liad for the term of my own marriage, through the child's birth."

"And thus may stand in my place, should urgent business of the clan arise. Yes. I believe it *will* answer–if you are satisfied now, sister, that the scheme will more likely benefit the child than harm him?"

"It is more than generous," Petrella said, with feeling. "I very much hope that it will result in a new pilot for yos'Phelium."

"If it does not," said Chi, rising and putting her glass next to Petrella's on the desk, "there will be your own child to take up the Ring when the time comes. Have we not already determined that yos'Galan, at least, breeds true?"

"Yes, but yos'Galan has no ambition to rise to delm," Petrella said quellingly.

"I understand. However, if yos'Galan produces a pilot and yos'Phelium does not, we will need to rearrange ambitions, as well as expectations."

She stretched.

"I'm away to dea'Gauss, and possibly yo'Lanna. Have you any errands I might dispatch for you in the city?"

"Thank you, no–no, stay! Where is Pilot pen'Uldra at the moment?"

"At the Pilot's Rest in Mid-Port. I hope to have him in less perilous conditions soon. Ilthiria may take him, once dea'Gauss has drafted the marriage lines."

"Assuming Justus agrees," said Petrella and Chi laughed.

"When has Ilthiria's lifemate stood against her?"

"There is that," Petrella said, and stood to open her arms.

Her sister stepped into the embrace, and then stepped away.

"Until soon, sister," she said.

"Until soon."

Petrella sighed, carried the wine glasses over to the buffet, and came back to her desk, frowning.

Something. . .there was something she was missing. Not Echieta, world of thieves that it was.

Not Telrune, certain.

Not–was it the boy's *name*?

pen'Uldra.

She sat down at the desk, frowning.

pen'Uldra.

There had been. . .*surely* there had been. . .

She reached to the screen, and called up the *Encyclopedia of Trade*.

pen'Uldra.

III

Fer Gun pen'Uldra sat in the little sunroom that had become his favorite corner at Glavda Empri. He had been the guest of Lady yo'Lanna long enough now that it no longer seemed. . .very strange that the house–the structure–had its own name, as if it were a ship or some other nobler thing than a place to sleep and sup.

Though to be sure, Glavda Empri housed many, entertained more, and was older itself then Clan Telrune. Mayhap it had earned its own name.

He shook out his ruffles and settled himself in the chair. Go back twelve days and he could have said with perfect truth that he had never worn ruffles in his life. Now, he possessed several shirts–made to his own size!–in various colors, each of them showing lace at cuff and collar. In the usual way of things, so he had lately learned, a gentleman did not wear lace in the daytime, or, unless expecting visitors, in the privacy of his own parlor.

But, said Lady yo'Lanna, he had so short a time to learn the way of them, that it must be ruffles and full dress coat throughout the day.

He feared that he would never learn the way of ruffles, though he had marked that there had been less corrections to his manner over the last two days. Perhaps he had gained some proficiency, after all.

That, he thought was more likely than the possibility that Lady yo'Lanna had given him up as a hopeless case. After a relumma in her care, he had *her* measure at least–and she was not a woman who accepted defeat. Also, she was Chi yos'Phelium's especial friend; and she had promised that she would deliver an unexceptionable spouse-elect to the signing.

So it was that he had language lessons, and deportment lessons, and dancing lessons. He was given several fat chapters of the Code to sleep-learn so that he might discuss them with his hostess over mid-morning tea, and so fix them in his mind.

It was, he admitted, gazing out over the garden that seemed to have no outward boundary, an unusual and demanding, curriculum. He had never been an avid scholar; even at Anlingdin he had cared for nothing beyond his piloting lessons, deeming the rest of his courses distractions from the real business he had come to learn.

And, atop his new clothes, and his new manner, he had also achieved grooming. Nothing would make his hair amenable and smooth, but the barber summoned by Lady yo'Lanna had clipped the thick stuff short on the sides, and swept it away from his face, while leaving the crown and back longer, so that it almost *seemed* his own hair, though shockingly free of elf-locks.

Even Lady yo'Lanna had been pleased with the results. At least, he supposed that, "Yes, I thought that you would dress well," conveyed pleasure.

Of all the persons he had met over this twelve-day, and there had been a surprising number of them, he had seen his wife-to-be only once, and that in company with a very worthy city-man who had been introduced as "Mr. dea'Gauss, my man of business. He will be writing the contracts."

They had then gotten immediately down to details, presented with perfect clarity by Mr. dea'Gauss: In return to his service to Korval, Fer Gun pen'Uldra Clan Telrune would receive a sum of five cantra, to be delivered to his hand on-signing. His daily expenses and reasonable others, for the duration of the contract, would be borne by Clan Korval. Should eighteen months elapse and best efforts had not resulted in a child, the contract would be considered ended, and he would receive the remainder of his fee. Clan Telrune would receive a sum totaling his expected earnings as a first class pilot for the term of the contract, payable to them when the contract was complete. Telrune, dea'Gauss assured him, had accepted those terms, without question, which Fer Gun doubted not at all. The marriage-portion was free money to Telrune, and only a fool would turn it down, or endanger its arrival by scheming for more.

So, the marriage contract.

There had been a second contract, much more complex, and he had understood that it would likely not be complete before the marriage was made.

That contract. . .he smiled in anticipation, and did not allow himself to consider that she would withhold it, once she had him married. He had, he told himself, already agreed to the marriage; there had been no necessity to offer–

"Ah, I thought I might find you here," Lady yo'Lanna said briskly, startling him out of what he supposed must have been a doze.

"It's quite the most pleasant room in the house, isn't it?" she continued, coming 'round to sit in the chair across from him. She had a courier envelope in one hand and a pen in the other.

"You will be glad to see this, I warrant, Pilot," she said, offering the envelope and the pen. "I am told that this is the draft of the marriage lines for your review. If all is well, you are to initial it in the place indicated and return it to dea'Gauss."

He opened the envelope; somewhat dismayed by the number of pages. Still, he knew from experience that paperwork was complicated, even when the agreement was simple.

There was a bright green clip on the next-to-last page. He flipped the packet open to the the spot, turning to place it on the chair-side table, as he uncapped the pen and –

"Stop this moment!" Lady yo'Lanna said sharply.

He blinked, and turned his head to look at her, pen poised over paper.

"Have you read that contract?" she demanded.

"No," he admitted. "But we spoke–myself, and Pilot Chi, and *Qe'andra* dea'Gauss. All agreed what ought to be in it."

"And so you will sign it blind?" she demanded. "How do you know that there is not a paragraph in that contract which states, should you indeed provide a pilot to Korval, that you will be kept at stud for the next twelve years?"

He stared at her.

"Pilot Chi –" he began.

She held up a hand, freezing the words in his throat.

"Chi yos'Phelium is my dearest and oldest friend. She is also Korval. Chi certainly would do no such thing. But Korval is a very different matter. *She* will do what she must for the clan. And you will do well to remember, young Fer Gun, that it is *Korval* who produced the basis of that draft, after the three of you had your discussions."

Fer Gun took a breath. His stomach, he noted distantly, was. . .unsettled.

"You will sit there, and you will read that contract, word by word, and line by line" Lady yo'Lanna told him. "I will not permit you to sully *my melant'i* by doing otherwise." She rose, and looked down her nose at him.

"You will do well to take it as a life-lesson, Pilot pen'Uldra: *Always* read the contract. Always *understand* the contract. I will return here in an hour, and I will expect to be told the terms of that document. If you should have questions, or find that there are provisions you do not understand, make a note of them so that you may inquire either of our clan's *qe'andra*, or another of your choosing."

Fer Gun swallowed.

"Yes, ma'am," he said. There was no other possible answer.

Lady yo'Lanna inclined her head.

"I will send tea," she said, and left him.

IV

"You must admit," said an overly cheerful voice just beyond the dressing room where Fer Gun stood, staring at the stranger in the mirror and wishing very much to be anywhere else.

"What do I have to admit?" he asked, around a queasy stomach.

Lady yo'Lanna's brother, Lord ter'Meulen, had taken an active part in Fer Gun's education. Where the lady was incisive and inclined to scold, her brother was light-speaking, unflappable, and unserious. Well. That was the impression he wished to give, at least. Fer Gun was fairly certain that, in the extremely unlikely event that he was seen to pose a threat, he would find his lordship wearing a very different face.

As Fer Gun was no threat, and ter'Meulen well aware of it, the face he saw was amused and a little sardonic. His lordship was every bit as informative as his sister, though of a slightly different flavor. If the lady's preferred topic was form, her brother's was function.

"You have to admit," his lordship said now, strolling into the dressing room, "that Chi has an eye for a well-looking man. Ilthiria doubted that you would clean up more than passably well, but look at you! You might be the *na'delm* of some off-world High House."

"Or I might be a wingless pilot from a clan so low neither Korval nor Guayar can see us on a clear day."

ter'Meulen's eyebrows rose slightly.

"Dismay gives you an edge, I see. Take my advice and keep your knives close. Soft words, and few, will win this day for you. If Korval had decided upon full formal, and all the High and High Mid-Houses in attendance, then, my child, you would have needed all the knives in your arsenal, and all that I could lend you."

Lady yo'Lanna had very carefully explained to him that the event surrounding the signing of the lines was small, scarcely more than tea with friends. Which, he conceded, it might well seem to one who had known the attendees for all of her life. For him–well, he was the two-headed calf, as Jai Kob would have it: an oddity with only one thing to recommend him.

He turned to face Lord ter'Meulen, letting the reflection of the stranger in his fine clothes and jewels slide out of sight.

"Why does Korval make the signing public at all?" he asked, a question that had only lately occurred to him, as all of his informants had simply spoken of the signing and the luncheon as an accomplished fact. "It is only a contract marriage, after all. We might sign the lines in *Qe'andra* dea'Gauss' office."

"Ah, has no one bothered to tell you? That was ill-done of us. We are well-versed in the reasons, but they are far from a universal interest."

He walked over to the bureau, where someone had left a tray holding six glasses and a pitcher.

"Cold mint tea?" he asked. "It will settle your stomach." He poured a glass, and inclined his head. "And mine."

That must have been meant as a jest, Fer Gun thought. *ter'Meulen* wasn't about to be married before of a room full of strangers, all of whom would see through the fine feathers he had been lent, to the molting magpie beneath.

"Truly," ter'Meulen said, turning to look at him. "The tea will do you good."

"Thank you, then," Fer Gun said with ill grace, and moved forward to receive the glass. "She had told me that she needs a child who will grow to be a pilot, as the elder child has proven unfit, but –"

Lord ter'Meulen raised his hand, his face in the moment very nearly stern.

"The elder child is brilliant, and convenable, and an asset to her House. Merely, she is not a pilot, and Korval House law states that the delm must be a pilot."

Fer Gun felt his face heat. He bowed.

"I meant no insult to the lady. Forgive my awkward tongue."

His lordship awarded him a broad smile, all displeasure vanished.

"There! *That* is the mode–sweet and soft-spoken. Now, the answer to your question is this: yos'Phelium is the delm's Line. As Kareen cannot stand na'delm, and Chi unwisely placed all of her coins on that one cast of the dice, she must now scramble for an heir. And she must do so as publicly as possible, to put to rest any rumor that this second child's claim is illegitimate."

Fer Gun had a sip of tea, which was pleasantly cool in a parched mouth.

"She had said that Festival-get would not serve her purpose," he recalled.

"The least attractive solution, though it may yet be brought to the board, should Korval wish to fill the nurseries against need. That, of course, is Korval's decision."

ter'Meulen sipped from his glass.

"There is another child. Sae Zar yos'Galan is a pilot and so might be delm, but he is yos'Galan's heir, and will be the clan's master trader, in his time. There are no more children behind him, either. So we come to the current solution, which is that yos'Galan will contract-wed–that happy event has already taken place–and yos'Phelium also. This will produce two children – the na'delm and an extra. The best outcome is that both children will prove to be pilots. The lesser, but acceptable, outcome is that one will be a pilot, and so Korval will have a delm. If neither child is a pilot. . ."

His lordship shrugged.

"But, why is Korval so few?" Fer Gun blurted, recalling Telrune's house, overfull with cousins, and never lacking for babies.

ter'Meulen sipped his tea, and put the glass aside

"That is a question best put to Chi. I can recite facts, but you will want reasons, and those I cannot give you." He cocked his head.

"Finish your tea, child. It's time we were off."

* * *

Chi took one last look around the contract room. The flowers twined prettily up the bed posts, their fragrance subtly scenting the room. Light flowed sweetly in to the room from the wide window that overlooked the inner garden.

Of course, she ought to have used the contract room overlooking the formal gardens at the front of the house, but the inner garden was, in her opinion, a pleasanter prospect, and smaller, which might, perhaps, comfort a boy who had been accustomed to limited sight-lines even before he had taken to ships.

The contract-room having proved itself agreeable, Chi crossed to the door in the right-hand wall, opened it and stepped into the room that would be occupied by Fer Gun pen'Uldra for the small time that he would actually be residing in the house. After the business of the contract-room was completed, he would retire here, to sleep, or pursue what other activities might beguile him. Again, she had attempted to make it agreeable to the sensibilities of a boy of humble means. There was a comfortably worn sofa and a well-broken in chair near the fireplace, and a modest offering of real bound books on the shelves. Over near the window, was the desk, the screen useful for either entertainment or work. She had also had a scanner placed on the desk, so he might listen to the business of the port.

The kitchenette was reasonably well supplied with wine and tea and small foods, such as one might wish for of an evening while one sat with a book, or an afternoon snack in front of a work screen.

The sleeping room was adequate without being opulent. There was a soft rug underfoot, and a sky-window over the bed. An extremely modest jewel box, sufficient to accommodate the lad's extremely modest jewels, sat atop a plain, six-drawer dresser. There were clothes in the closet–not very many, and tailored as simply as could be managed while still preserving elegance and style.

It would, she decided, do. Indeed, it would have to do. And, after all, the lad had spent a relumma in one of Glavda Empri's guesting suites. Perhaps he had acquired a taste for elegance.

She returned to the contract room, being careful to close the door to the spouse's quarters firmly behind her, and opened the door in the left-hand wall.

This would be her apartment while the contract was in force; not very much more luxurious than its opposite on the other side of the contract room. After all, they would not be on Liad above a day or two before removing to *Comet* and lifting in pursuit of their new-signed business venture.

She owned herself to be looking forward to the small introductory trip. Liad became tiresome after a while, with its *melant'i* games and intrigues. The challenges of piloting, and even of establishing a base-line for a new route to be run by a new captain, were charmingly straightforward, and even refreshing, by comparison.

A glance at the small clock on the bookshelf told her that was closing in on the hour.

She would soon be wanted downstairs. The guests would have arrived by now, received by Petrella; and Bal Dyn ter'Meulen would be arriving soon, her spouse-to-be in hand.

She tarried a moment, yet, considering that spouse-to-be. A rough lad, scantily tutored. She did not expect that he had been given any bed-lessons beyond what had been learned from such lovers as he may have had. And, truly, it scarcely mattered if the lad merely lay there and left all the details fell to her. The point of the exercise being, not an enjoyment of art, or of each other, but simple, even coarse biology.

A child, of her body. A pilot, if the genes aligned, to lead the next generation of Korval.

And, if yos'Phelium had played out at last, then best to *let* the Line die, and leave yos'Galan free to marry another Line less likely to draw catastrophe upon it and all its workings.

The small clock chimed the hour.

Chi yos'Phelium sighed lightly, squared her shoulders, and took herself downstairs to be married.

#

Kareen met her at door to the small gather-room, all proper and smooth-faced. Chi did not sigh. Kareen was inclined to the opinion that Korval clan law was outmoded and required revision to bring it into modern times. She was further of the opinion that adhering to a protocol made in the last universe during a time of war and strife did active harm to a clan residing in a time and universe of relative peace and prosperity.

She was not, as Chi had admitted, entirely wrong in either of those assessments. However, there was a contract to keep, and to that, once shown the terms, not even Kareen had an answer.

"Mother." Her eldest bowed and offered an arm, which Chi took gently.

"Daughter," she answered. "I am grateful for your guidance."

It was only partly a joke; she *was* grateful that Kareen had agreed to be her support at the signing–and not merely because it would involve her personally, and perhaps reconcile her to the inevitable.

If she did not actively frown, nor did Kareen smile; she merely stepped across the threshold and into the room.

The clamor of voices softened somewhat as they entered, and not a few pair of eyes followed them on their way to the small dais, where her sister waited.

"You are just in time," Petrella said, leaning close to kiss her cheek.

"So long as I am not late," she answered, and allowed Kareen to assist her onto the stage.

She took up her position behind the table, to the left of the portfolio and the pens, Kareen standing one step to the rear and the right.

Those who had watched her progress turned back to their interrupted conversations. The sound of voices swelled–and all at once went silent.

Bal Dyn ter'Meulen, whose instincts *never* failed him, paused on the threshold, head up, face calm, and allowed the room to look their fill, not of him. . .

. . .but of the young man on his arm.

Oh, thought Chi, looking as well–Ilthiria, whose instincts perhaps surpassed even her brother's, had risen above all of her past perfections in the dressing of the spouse.

A dark blue coat with a deep nap that showed subtle pinpoints of silver when the boy moved. A white shirt, modestly ruffled down the front, as pure as a child's honor. The ruffles at his wrists were deep, falling softly over hands that were no strangers to hard labor; a ring set with a dark blue stone flashed shyly on his right hand, and the dark trousers accentuated long, shapely legs.

He was not, Chi thought, considering the guests, anything like what had been expected. They had expected outworld manners, graceless, if not crude, but this–finely dressed and haughty, like a dagger in a velvet sheathe–took them back a step. He stood straight and utterly cool, his arm linked with that of his escort, his face composed and even cold; eyes like black diamonds glittering beneath heavy dark lashes.

Very likely the child was terrified, Chi thought, but if so, those gathered were not know it. Indeed, she thought, watching the pair of them approach the stage unimpeded, as one after another stepped aside to let them pass–Indeed, it would seem that Fer Gun pen'Uldra's whole purpose was deny those gathered the spectacle of his fear.

There was not the least bit of awkwardness at the dais, and Fer Gun took his place, unhurried and deliberate, behind the table, at the right of the portfolio and pen, while Bal Dyn stood one step behind and to the right, witness to the proceedings.

The crowd parted once more, and Mr. dea'Gauss stepped forward. He walked up to, but did not mount, the dais, and turned to face those gathered.

"We are here to witness the signing of the contract of engenderment made between Chi yos'Phelium Clan Korval and Fer Gun pen'Uldra Clan Telrune, with the child coming to Clan Korval."

You might have heard a speck of dust fall onto the floor; it seemed that no one in the room dared breathe.

"We begin," said Mr. dea'Gauss gravely. "Fer Gun pen'Uldra Clan Telrune, please affix your name to the contract."

#

"Lady yos'Galan, a moment of your time, if you please."

Petrella turned to consider the society page editor for the Gazette, Finlee as'Barta.

"Certainly, ma'am," she said, watching out of the corner of her eye as Chi maneuvered her contract-husband toward a knot of stalwart friends of Korval. "How may I assist you?"

"I would value some insight into who, precisely, Fer Gun pen'Uldra Clan Telrune is," Editor as'Barta said crisply.

Petrella raised an eyebrow.

"Surely, the Book of Clans. . ."

"I have, I assure you, perused the Book of Clans. It reveals to me that Clan Telrune is seated upon Echieta, a world which appears to exist to offer repairs to ships in. . .reduced circumstances. It is, perhaps, an unsavory world; nor does Clan Telrune appear to stand high among those Clans seated there."

"Alas, there are many such worlds, and stations, as Echieta, which pursue their lives as they find best, away from the luminous oversight of the homeworld," Petrella said, perhaps not as gently as she might have done. Indeed, the editor's lips parted. Petrella raised her hand, and spoke on.

"Your question, however, has to do with the personal history of yos'Phelium's contracted spouse. Fer Gun pen'Uldra is the grandson and only surviving heir of Arl Fed pen'Uldra, who had been for many years an influence in the so-called Divers Trade Association. He served two terms as one of the twelve seated commissioners–six Liaden, and six Terran–and served also for many years as one of the twenty-four ombudsman, as well as standing Thirteenth–the tie-breaking vote – for three cycles of the council.

"At one time, Arl Fed pen'Uldra owned, with his lifemate, a fleet of four small traders."

Finlee as'Barta stared at her.

"I would ask for documentation, as the Book of Clans has failed me."

"The information is largely found in the trade histories. It will be my pleasure to send the cites to you."

"I thank you. One does wonder what became of the traderships, the grandfather, and the spouse's parents."

"The tale turns bitter, I fear," Petrella said. "This information will of course be included in the cites. In short, the success of the Divers Trade Association made its members targets of pirates and other unsavory persons. Captain pen'Uldra lost his ships, his lifemate, and his children. With the one grandchild remaining to him not yet a Standard old, he sought refuge with his cousins in Clan Telrune, the better to hide the child from those who would murder him for his birthright. Captain pen'Uldra died very soon after going to ground on Echieta, and the child, now yos'Phelium's spouse, was raised by Telrune."

"A touching history," Editor as'Barta murmured. "Pilot pen'Uldra is fortunate that Korval was aware of his circumstances. Of course, he is a pilot to behold?"

"By all accounts, he is," Petrella acknowledged.

"Which must of course, Korval being Korval, carry all before it."

Editor as'Barta turned to survey Chi and her spouse, who were receiving congratulations from Azia pel'Otra Clan Elarnt, a solid trading family long affiliated with Korval in general and yos'Galan in particular.

"Quite young, too," as'Barta said, which was merely spite, "and one, assumes, easily guided."

"That has not been my experience of the pilot," Petrella answered sweetly.

"I must excuse myself," she said. "Be assured that I will send the cites to you this evening."

She bowed, and as'Barta did, and Petrella walked away, seething, to greet the other guests.

* * *

It was done.

Well, no, Fer Gun corrected himself; the signing and the reception, and the displaying of manners only recently learned to persons he had never thought to meet, even if he had known of their existence–*that* was done. He hoped he did not flatter himself, to think that it had been done, if not well, at least credibly.

He had found it. . .astonishingly easy to fall into Lord ter'Meulen's suggested mode of soft-voiced modesty, and allow his spouse to carry all before her. It was entirely possible that he had learned some important and interesting things during his tour of the gather-room on Chi yos'Phelium's arm. His grandfather had told him that information was a coin with limited value, until it was paired with another, like, coin.

His grandfather had said other things, too, most of them doubtful, if not outright daft. But the importance of holding on to scraps of information until all the pieces came together to form a quilt–*that* Fer Gun had found to be apt. Trader Yinzatch aboard *Selich* where he'd hired on directly after school–Trader Yinzatch held to a similar understanding of data and its relationships, and had in addition been a wizard in matching edges. It had been an education to watch the trader at work, even for a pilot.

For now, though. . .

For now, he was at liberty, having been shown to the apartment which was to be his during the time he guested in Korval's house–another named as if it were a ship: Jelaza Kazone.

They were pleasant rooms, much less grand than those he had lived in at Glavda Empri, which was, he admitted to himself, a relief.

He took some moments to explore, after he had removed his loaned finery, and placed the ring and earrings into the plain box atop the dresser. He frowned on finding several rings, and earrings, a handful of jeweled pins, and glittering chains in the box when he opened it. He took a breath, to cool the flicker of temper. The contract, he reminded himself, stipulated that he might be required to attend several more gathers in support of his spouse. It would not show well on her, if he appeared each time in the same coat–which was why there were six made in his size hanging in the closet. It would show equally ill on her, if he repeated today's jewels–or wore those which were his in truth–a pair of silver earrings set with ruby, which his grandfather had told him had belonged to his mother, and a silver bracelet which had, according to grandfather, belonged to his mother's mother.

After he had explored the apartment, he looked in the tiny kitchen. He had eaten little at the luncheon, and only sipped the wine, feeling the need to have such wits as he owned well about him. Nor had he done justice to the breakfast he had been offered at Glavda Empri.

He ought, he reasoned, be hungry; it had been a long day and difficult, and by no means over, yet. A perusal of the various small foods and vintages in the kitchen, however, failed to turn up anything that tempted, and in the end he drew a glass of cold water, and went to stand in the window, and look down at a tangle of vegetation through which a slender walk could barely be seen.

He knew little about growing things or gardens. The disorder of this one appealed to him, though, and he was drawn to the colors of the many flowers.

He glanced upward, but the angle of the window foiled any sighting of Korval's Tree, the top of which he could see quite clearly from his rooms at Glavda Empri.

After a time, his water finished, he left the window, and glanced to the bookcase, not so that he might know which titles were available to him, but that he might see the small clock set on one of the shelves.

His stomach tightened, and his chest cramped. In an hour, he was to meet his wife in the contract-room, there to perform such duties as had been lain out in the contract.

Deliberately, he closed his eyes, and ran one of the mental exercises which were taught to pilots, to ensure that their minds were clear and their energy levels high.

His breathing smoothed; his muscles relaxed.

Yes, he told himself, that's more the mode; it's a risky flight, but you'll do well so long as you mind your board.

Well.

With another glance at the clock, he went to ready himself for duty.

#

He arrived in the contract room early, so not to keep his wife waiting–which was respectful, according to the sections of Code Lady yo'Lanna had him Learn, and then discussed with him over the morning meal, in order to set the material in his mind.

Respectful it may have been, but it did nothing for his nerves to be alone with the ornate bed, a living vine growing up the posts and across the headboard, the flowers nodding heavily and giving up their scent to the room.

He regretted now, his failure to eat; he had wanted to keep a clear head, but the flowers would have him muddled before ever the business was well underway.

Stepping away from the bed, he opened the window, filling his lungs with cool air lightly scented with loam and green growing things and flowers of a. . .less complex nature.

He leaned closer into the window, closed his eyes–and snapped upright, eyes open, as he heard a door open.

Chi yos'Phelium, his contracted wife, glided silently toward him on naked feet. She wore, as he did, a long silk robe, belted at the waist. His robe was black, painted red flowers extending from his left shoulder, across his chest, down, and all around the hem. Her robe was green, patterned with small blue birds–or small blue dragons–and the belt was tied loosely, indeed.

He swallowed, hard, and recalled himself, a bare relumma in the past, rough and angry in a low port bar, thinking that *certainly* he would bed the elder pilot, if she was prepared to buy herself some fun, and maybe he would keep her on his string, too, since he'd had no other means to eat.

That Fer Gun pen'Uldra, he thought now, had been an idiot. A swaggering port-tough who had no idea of *real* danger.

This Fer Gun pen'Uldra, contracted to give the fine elder pilot before him a child. . .recognized every one of his failings in an instant; his lack of finesse or any other bed-skill, save, perhaps, endurance, and even that, he thought, as she crossed the room like a tigress, might fall before her.

She was well to look upon, too. *Elder pilot* indeed, he sneered at his past idiot self. Oh, she was older than he was, in years, in guile, in polish. She might undertake to teach him his own name, and he would learn from her lesson. He was not her match–not near her match, in any thing–and it was far more likely that she would have kept a brash pilot on her string for exactly so long as she had use for him, had their first meeting gone as he had predicted, and cast him away with nothing when she was done.

The green robe clung to every line of her long, strong frame. The skin revealed by the loosened knot was pure gold, and so smooth his fingers, still rough despite Lady yo'Lanna's lotions, would surely catch and scratch her.

She came to stand beside him, and turned her face to the window, smiling into the soft breeze.

"The inner court at this hour is splendid, is it not?" she said in the comfortable mode of comrade.

"The breeze is refreshing," he offered in turn, marking the unsteadiness in his own voice.

"That it is," she said, apparently noting nothing amiss.

She stepped slightly away from the window, turning so that they faced each other.

"I have a gift for you," she said; "may I give it?"

His victory was that he did not look immediately at what the robe revealed, but kept his eyes on hers.

"I. . .have no gift for you," he said, around a feeling of strong dismay. The giving of contract-room gifts had not been among those customs he had Learned. Had he given offense already? Perhaps it might soothe the feelings of his past self, that at least it had not been for his performance in bed.

"There is no reason why you should have any gift for me, other than yourself," Chi yos'Phelium was saying, with a smile. "It is a whim–I fear that you will find me whimsical."

She paused, head tipped to one side.

"May I give the gift?"

He drew a breath, seeking calm, and managed to meet her smile with one of his own.

"Yes, please."

"Excellent."

She raised the hand she had kept slightly behind her; he took the card from between slim fingers–and only just managed to swallow a curse.

"My license!" he said, staring at her.

She raised her eyebrows.

"Is the gift inept?"

He drew a breath, folding his hand around the card in sudden fear that she might snatch it back. Whimsical, indeed.

"The gift is appreciated," he said choosing his words with as much care as he was able. "But, Pilot–I was to have stood, wingless, a year. At the end of our contract, you had promised to come with me to the Guild and speak for my good name. That," he concluded, somewhat breathlessly, "was the agreement."

"Well, so it was," she said. "But you will need your license and your wings if we are to take our partnership forward in the matter of the small trader, and so I put the matter before the Guild Master. He was much struck."

She bought your card back for you, Fer Gun told himself. Gods alive, she *bribed* the Guild Master. He ought to have cared, indeed, the risk of it chilled him, but very nearly all of his thought was for the license in his hand, which he would not relinquish again for anything he could name.

"We also reviewed the matter which had brought you to the attention of the Port Proctors and so the Guild," Chi said, turning toward the small table that held a pitcher of wine and a plate of cheeses and small breads.

Fer Gun swallowed.

"And?" he said.

Her eyebrows rose again.

"Why, the Guild Master agreed that your cousins are very clever. Will you have wine?"

He blinked. That was twice she had commented on the cleverness of his cousins. There was something there, and he too thickheaded to see it–and the lady had asked him a question.

"Wine," he said careful again. "I would prefer not. The flowers. . ."

The flowers were making him queasy, and his head was beginning to ache with their stench. If he was to do her any good at all this night. . .

"Ah."

She inclined her head.

"They are rather insistent, are they not?" she said and walked past him to push the window wide.

Pausing there, she looked down in to the garden, then turned again to face him.

"I should like to go for a walk in the garden," she said. "It is my habit of an evening, and I have not had an opportunity, amid all the brangle and the bowing. How if you put your ticket safely away, and accompany me? It is a very fine garden, despite its disreputable habit."

"I –" he stammered to a halt. "What does one wear, to ramble through a garden at night?"

She glanced down at herself, and then to him.

"These will do," she said. "Will you come?"

"Yes," he said, and bowed. "I will only be a moment."

* * *

It was much pleasanter in the garden than inside, Chi thought; and the lad–she stopped herself. She needed to stop thinking of him in quite that way. Yes, she could give him a dozen years or more–yet he was a man grown, who held a Jump pilot's license, and had managed, against considerable odds to the contrary, to survive his childhood, the death of his sole protector, and the particular attentions of his so-clever cousins.

Thrust into a game the rules of which he could not hope to master, yet he had managed to keep himself in good order, without exposing vulnerability or weakness to those who might be expected to exploit such things. He had *learnt* the lessons he had been set to, and Ilthiria had not spared him, for either his youth or his upbringing.

"Who cares for all of these?" he asked now.

She glanced over to him–very nearly, he matched her own height, a novelty of its own–and moved her shoulders.

"In theory, I do," she said, wry in the face of his earnestness. "In truth, there is Master Gardner Byneta with whom I confer, and who will occasionally allow me to weed out a planting, but does not, I fear, quite trust me with a landscape knife."

He frowned at her.

"You were a scout, Lady yo'Lanna told me."

"Oh, indeed. A captain of scouts, as it came about, and to the astonishment of everyone, including myself."

"Then you're surely safe with a landscape knife," he pursued.

She grinned.

"As you know and I know. However, those who recall the days when one was scarcely safe with a rubber ball, and liable to stab one's own hand with a butter knife. . ."

She smiled, inviting him to acknowledge the joke, and after a moment had pleasure of seeing a smile that actually reached those space-black eyes, and very nearly thawed them.

"In any case, it is Master Byneta who cares for the garden, as I do not dare go against her wishes."

The path they were following all but disappeared beneath an overgrown bank of viburnum. She stepped ahead of him, slipping her hand into his as she passed. She felt his fingers twitch in shock, but he did not withdraw, and she tugged him after her, around the path's last curve, and into the Tree Court.

She paused at the very end of the path to allow him to see what it was he approached. His hand, she kept firmly in hers and he did not withdraw, nor even seem to know that they were linked.

Herself, she felt the Tree's regard focus upon her and a greenly sense of welcome. Excellent, her throw had not gone awry.

"Korval's Tree," she said, quietly, to her husband. "My favorite place in all the inner garden."

"It is less grown over, here," Fer Gun said, soft-voiced, as if he sensed something sleeping and did not wish to wake it. "But. . .more wild."

"That would be the Tree's influence," she said. "It likes its comfort, be certain of that, and makes certain that all and everything in this court is arranged to its best liking. Come, let us introduce you."

She stepped forward, walking carefully over the surface roots, the grass cool and damp against naked feet. He came willingly, still with his hand in hers.

"You would introduce me to a. . .tree?" Fer Gun asked, when they had achieved the trunk and she had placed her hand palm first against the rough, warm bark.

"It likes to meet people," Chi told him. "There are not many new faces come to speak with it in the Tree Court, and it does not itself, you know, travel very well."

She heard a chuckle, then, and pleasant hearing it was, low and honestly amused.

"I can see that travel might present problems," he said. "What am I to do? Bow?"

"Indeed not. Merely put your hand, so, against the trunk, and let us see what will happen."

* * *

The garden breeze brought immediate relief to his aching head and queasy stomach. He considered the plants that grudgingly allowed their passage along the stone walk with grateful benevolence. It occurred to him that he had not been at ease–truly at ease–since he had been picked up by the Port Proctors for holding a piece of paper for his cousin Jai Kob, and thereby lost his wings.

And hadn't the ship spun three hundred sixty degrees on its axis, when that event, which had been the low point of his life, was now revealed to be his most fortunate moment?

The path narrowed again, and Chi stepped ahead of him, light-foot. He felt a warm hand slip 'round his, caught his breath–and let it out in a sigh.

Hand-clasped, he followed her round a pile of living green very nearly as tall as he was, which had put forth round blue flowers easily as big as his head.

On the other side of the bush, the path vanished, and he came to rest next to his wife on the edge of what looked to be a public park, the grass short and well-tended, and the space open. Roses rioted on edge of the clearing and to the right there was a bench placed before them. In the center of the clearing, though, was an enormous trunk. He craned his head back, and sighted along it.

Korval's Tree.

"You would introduce me to a tree?" he asked, though, really, the notion scarcely seemed out of the way, given the very presence of the Tree. He was very conscious of Chi's hand in his, and of the fact that the breeze in this enclosed place was slightly brisker than out in the wider garden. Wisps of blonde hair had been teased out of the loose knot at Chi's nape, and he was suddenly taken with the notion of sliding his hands into her hair, becoming complicit in its disorder; and placing his lips against the soft skin of her throat.

Her hand tightened 'round his and she led him forward, to the very Tree itself.

"What shall I do?" he asked her. "Bow?"

"Indeed not. Merely put your hand, so, against the trunk, and let us see what happens."

He did as she said, pressing his unencumbered hand flat against the bark.

It was rough, and surprisingly warm. He felt a wave of–of happiness?–crash into and through him, and he was so delighted that he threw back his head and laughed aloud.

He heard Chi laugh, also, through the racket of happiness, and felt her hand still warm in his. From somewhere, he heard the sound of leaves snapping, and, obedient to the prompting of the joyful presence all about, he stepped back, and raised his free hand, palm up.

Next to him, Chi had done the same, and they each caught a round, green. . .seed pod, he thought. . .at the same instant.

The uproaring welcome faded, leaving him bouyed with anticipation, he turned, to see her eyes sparkling; the loosened tendrils of her hair moving softly about her face, scandalously stroking cheeks and brow and. . .

He swallowed and brought the pod up.

"What is this?"

"This," she announced, sounding as breathlessly delighted as he felt, "is a rare treat indeed! I wager you have never had the like. Here –"

She held her hand up, showing him the pod on her palm. Perhaps she blew on it. Perhaps she had squeezed it when she'd caught it.

In any case, the pod merely. . .fell open, revealing a nut nestled in each quarter.

"We eat them," she said, and without further explanation, slipped a portion of nut into her mouth.

He looked down at his hand, to find that his pod, too, had fallen open, and the aroma of the nuts made him realize all his hunger at once.

He all but snatched up the first piece, managing not to cram it into his mouth. It was–he had never. . .

It was perfect.

He ate the second piece, and it, too, was perfection; as was the third.

The fourth. . .he hesitated, and looked into her brilliant blue eyes.

"This," he said, holding it toward her; "is yours."

She smiled and raised her hand.

"And this," she murmured, "is yours."

She stepped forward, and he did, each lifting the treat to the other's lips. Warmth filled him, and surety; his loins were beyond warm, and he stepped forward again, or she did. He thrust his fingers into the silly knot, freeing silken strands for the breeze to make merry with, as he bent to press his mouth to the base of her throat, feeling her fingers tracing down his chest, and his robe–her robe. . .Gods, she felt so good.

She made a soft growling sound, and pulled his head down to her breast.

* * *

Some time later, they lay together at the base of the Tree, the grass as soft as any mattress while they learned each other, and learned themselves, and cried out in joyous release.

Chi woke. . .later, to find the Tree park filled with a gentle glow, and a blanket of leaves cast over them like a quilt. Fer Gun lay with his head on her breast, and she was of no mind to move him, or to rise and go into the house.

She settled her chin atop his head, closed her eyes. Above them, the wind moved through the leaves in a lullaby.

Chi went back to sleep.

V

The good ship *Comet*, out of Chonselta, Liad, belied her name somewhat, erring on the side of dependable and everyday, rather than on flash and glitter. She was patient with two pilots who continually tried her, teasing out her strengths and her limits; unapologetic when they confirmed that she was not a scout ship, for they had also found that she was not a garbage scow. A working small trader, that was all and everything that she claimed to be, and that was, in fact, exactly what she was.

Pilot Fer Gun pen'Uldra proved to be something other than Chi had had anticipated, given his scores, his Guild test ratings, and his speed. Oh, he was everything that was quick and knowing at the board–that she had expected. But she had not expected Fer Gun pen'Uldra to be patient with the limits of so pedestrian a vessel. She had, in fact, rather rather thought that he would chafe under those limits, perhaps show a bit of temper, and even some disdain for work-a-day *Comet*, so far beneath his abilities.

Instead, he fair crooned over her, and gave her fulsome praise when she held her line and refused to be intimidated by the demands of an extended run at the top of her range.

"She won't let us down, this lady," he told Chi. They had finally gotten done with testing and trying and got themselves on the way to Mondaw. *Comet* had gone into Jump with nary a complaint nor a bobble, all boards green and steady.

"She has heart," Chi agreed.

They were in the galley, sharing a celebratory cup of tea. Fer Gun was having a bowl of soup, too, while Chi contented herself with some salted crackers.

"We won't be picking up anything at Mondaw?" asked Fer Gun. "The whole reason is to meet this Vigro Welsh?"

"We are running podless, with two pilots the whole crew," Chi pointed out. "How much cargo can we take?"

"Small packages, and courier work," he said, lifting a shoulder. "Ships don't fly for free."

That was spacer economics, and true, so far as it went. Chi sipped her tea.

"We may find some small thing which needs to travel in our direction, but you will recall that the primary purpose of this trip, Captain pen'Uldra, is to introduce you to those firms and contacts with whom you will be working, once this ship is fully crewed and wearing her pods."

As he was still frowning, she added.

"Korval funds this tour as part of the cost of doing business."

"True enough, though it goes against the weave," he said, finishing his soup and rising to put the bowl in the washer. "Would you like more tea? Or something a little more to eat than two crackers?"

"By the time I am done here," she told him with dignity, "I will have had three crackers. And yes, I would like it if you would warm my tea."

He did so, and stood looking down at her. He was, she thought, much more suited to a ship than to Liad. It had been a wanton cruelty, to conspire so carefully to rob him of his wings. Though there always remained the possibility that the cousins had expected him to succumb to Low Port. She sighed, lightly. One would so treasure an opportunity to speak with the cousins.

Still...

"What are you thinking?" Fer Gun asked her. "Will Mondaw be a problem?"

That was a nicely reasoned leap, and phrased so that she need only answer one query.

"Mondaw ought to be nothing like a problem," she said, truthfully. "You have the files for review, do you not?"

He laughed.

"Do I not!" he repeated. "And I will set myself to reviewing them, again, I swear. In the meanwhile, you might have a nap."

She did *try* not to glare at him.

"Am I a fragile flower, Pilot?"

He traded her a stare for her glare. Those black eyes produced an admiral stare, indeed.

"The pilot requires the co-pilot to be able," he said. "You're tired. Even I can see that."

Chi bit back a sharp retort. After all, he was correct–she *was* tired, and would be the better for a rest. And he was twice correct to remind her of the progression of responsibilities, though she had learnt them before she could walk; there was a teaching rhyme that her nurse had sung to her.

The child being correct on both counts, she smiled up into those black, black eyes.

"I will, in fact, nap," she told him. "That is an excellent idea, Pilot."

* * *

Vigro Welsh was plain-spoken and hearty, and Mondaw something very like him. Fer Gun felt a cautious optimism. When this plan–this partnership–had first been proposed, he had had his doubts. Who would not have had doubts, partnered with Korval? *Comet* herself had been a reassurance–a ship in the common way, accustomed to the common work of ships, and nothing of the glittering luxury of Liad about her.

In the same way Vigro Welsh was reassuring–a merchant, who dealt in everyday wares, and presented no airs. He was comfortable in a matter-of-fact way that drew Fer Gun's envy. Where Glavda Empri, Jelaza Kazone, and Trealla Fantrol had discomforted and distressed him, Vigro Welsh's office and–nameless!–home was not only appealing, but seemed. . .attainable in a way that Chi's house would never be, for the likes of Fer Gun pen'Uldra.

There had been a tour of the warehouses, and introductions to various others of the Welsh network. The merchant's initial instinct had been to speak to Chi.

"Captain pen'Uldra will be regularly on the route," Chi said. "He will naturally be taking on a trader and crew. This stop is to make you known to each other, and so the captain may provide *Comet's* trader-to-be with current introductions."

That had set the merchant straight, and Fer Gun had found himself the center of a very sharp attention, indeed.

He was pleased to believe, at the end of the tour, after they had shared dinner at a local restaurant that was also in the network, that Vigro Welsh would not find himself embarrassed to be associated with Captain pen'Uldra and *Comet*. That left an unaccustomed warmth, which still buoyed him when then returned to the ship.

Once they were in and sealed, the two of them sat in the galley over wine, and talked through what they had seen, and he had learned, and considered those questions that he had.

When the debrief was done, he would have gone to his own quarters, but Chi had put her hand on his arm and smiled in that way that made his breath short and his blood warm. He had gone with her, therefore, and pleased he was to have done so.

#

It was next shift that trouble struck, though he thought nothing about it at the time. He'd risen, checked the comm, and the screens.

No messages for them on the overnight, but the screens showed a package sitting just over the line of their dock. A smallish package, easily carried in the courier hold, and it was such a common thing that he thought nothing of opening the hatch and walking out to pick it up.

He scanned it, naturally–he wasn't a *fool,* after all–and was on his way down the hall when the storm hatch snapped shut almost on his nose.

"What is that in your hand, Pilot?" Chi asked him over the intercom, her voice calm.

"A package," he said agreeably.

"Had we arranged for a package?" Chi asked, and it came to him, then, that her voice was not so much calm as *constrained.*

He frowned, suddenly and forcibly reminded of the studies she had had him make regarding lading slips, documents of transfer, the proper order and style of sign-offs.

"Had we," Chi asked again, "arranged for a package?"

"You know that we hadn't," he told her curtly. "I thought it had gotten kicked in."

There was a small silence, before she repeated, "Kicked in?"

A hasty, belated scan of the package showed no documentation, no bills, no stamps; none of the things that–that an *honest* package ought to have, leaving aside the detail that an honest package would have been openly delivered and signed for by the ship.

"When I was piloting for my cousins," he said, telling her the truth, no matter how badly it reflected on him. He had learned that: you told Chi yos'Phelium the truth, as plainly and as quickly as possible.

"When I was piloting for my cousins, it often happened that a package or a pallet was kicked inside our line, and was taken aboard as our rightful cargo." He hesitated, then finished the tale out, feeling an *utter* fool.

"We didn't have so much to do with lading slips, and tax stamps, and suchlike."

Silence for the count of twelve. He could feel the ice filling the corridor and wondered if he'd freeze to death, or if she'd only evacuate the air from the hallway.

"I am calling the port proctors," she said at last. "You will meet them on our dock and you will give that package to them. There will be questions; there may be forms to fill out. You will be everything that is convenable and forthright with the proctors, do you understand me, *Pilot*?"

The proctors. It fell on him, the memory of the proctors, the binders, the standing before Solcintra port security, and the Pilots Guild Master. The demand that he give over his license into the Guild's safekeeping. . .

It was on the edge of his tongue, then, to beg her to evacuate the hallway.

"The proctors are on their way," Chi said.

She would leave him here, gods, and he could scarcely blame her. However her means, she had redeemed his wings, and he repaid her with arrant stupidity.

He took a breath, and made sure his legs were steady enough to bear him before he bowed, in full sight of the camera–the bow of deep regret–before he turned toward the hatch and his doom.

#

"Eighth one this port-week," the elder of the two proctors said, who was clearly displeased, but not, it seemed at him.

Her partner finished scanning the package, produced a scan-proof bag from one of the many pouches on his belt and sealed the package inside.

"Inert," he said. "Like all the rest."

"And like all the rest, it will doubtless flash-bang when it's opened," the elder said. She looked to Fer Gun and bowed slightly.

"Our apologies, Pilot. This prank has been on-going. So far no harm has come of it, because the ships that dock at Mondaw are honest ships, and call the proctors immediately. We will need to take your statement, and we request a copy of your dock surveillance records. Perhaps we'll get lucky this time, and see a shadow."

For a moment, Fer Gun though his knees would give beneath his weight. A prank; an on-going prank, and he nothing more than its latest victim. The ship had behaved correctly, and the proctors had been called.

He wasn't going to be arrested, again. His license would remain in his pocket.

There would still be Chi yos'Phelium to deal with when this was over, but if she struck him dead on the spot for idiocy unbecoming a sentient, still, he would die a pilot.

"Certainly," he said to the proctors. "We will be pleased to share our records."

"Thank you, Pilot," the elder proctor said, and produced a note-taker from her belt. "Now, if you'll just tell me what happened, we'll add your testimony to the file."

* * *

The child was exhausted, Chi thought. Not surprising, really; terror did drain one's resources.

Now, he sat at the table in the galley, nursing his tea, and clearly waiting for doom to fall.

She sat across from him, and leaned her chin on her hand.

"I amend my opinion," she said, and smiled slightly when his eyes flew up to meet hers.

"Which opinion would that be?" he asked, his voice rough. "That in fact I am not naive, but stupid beyond redemption?"

Well. Here was angst. She had forgotten, almost, how very young he was.

"It was somewhat stupid to bring an undocumented package onto this ship," she said conversationally. "Though you were not so stupid that you failed to scan it. Habit is compelling, and we are all victims of our education. You have now, I believe, received an alternate education, and one that you will not soon forget. So, no, I have not changed my opinion of your abilities or potential."

"What then?" he asked, his voice less rough, and his face showing some ease.

"Well, I had been in the habit, as you know, of considering your cousins to be clever. I think now that they are not so much clever as very lucky. Did they never cheat anyone on the grey-fees?"

He blinked, and straightened somewhat in his chair.

"I was the pilot; not part of the dockside arrangements. Jai Kob had his contacts." He paused as if considering the matter fairly. "He also had Vin Dyr. Very few make progress against Vin Dyr."

"I see. They are then common port-toughs, with an amount of low cunning, but they are not, necessarily, clever. That is a fair judgment, I think, and I have no shame in altering my opinion of them. Now."

He winced slightly, and she smiled.

"I had been under the impression that you had known who your grandfather was. That may have been an error."

"Grandfather?" He frowned.

"My grandfather was old and ill and unsteady in his head. He came to rest at Telrune because no one else of his kin would take him."

"Ah," she said, and took a breath against a hot breath of anger.

"I will send some information to your screen," she said, rising. "We have several hours until lift, which should be sufficient for you to make yourself familiar with the data."

He rose, and bowed contrition.

"I will," he said, "try to. . .improve your opinion of me, Pilot."

"There's a worthy goal," she said lightly, and left him.

VI

They had set up their table on the hiring side of the Trade Hall on Dameeth, and had seen a suitably brisk business. There were some, so it seemed to Fer Gun, who altered their course to avoid when they saw the "Tree-and-Dragon Affiliate" card. That was well enough, in his opinion. It was no small thing, as he knew, to partner with Clan Korval. Such a partnership was more likely than not to change one's life, which was all very well for those like Fer Gun pen'Uldra, whose situation could only be changed for the better. Those who were satisfied with their lives, though–they did well to plot a course wide of Korval.

They had given five data-sticks, and collected three for review, which they would most assuredly do that evening on return to the ship. He had a favorite among the three, an elder trader with a steady air. Traveling with Chi yos'Phelium had taught him the value of a steady and knowledgeable elder. A new captain on a new route certainly would need all the steadiness and experience he could amass.

He scanned the room. It was edging toward the end of the day, and the hall was thinning. Those crewing the tables at either side of them were packing up to leave, their conversation all about dinner, and a glass or two of wine to aid the process of decision.

Indeed, he was on the edge of suggesting to Chi that they remove to review what they had collected, when a movement at the entrance to the hall drew his eye.

A trader had entered, walking with purpose down the line of hiring tables. She was tall, and wide-shouldered; her hair a smooth and glossy brown. Her clothes were respectable without being ostentatious, as had a few of the early applicants. Her single jewel was a garnet ring–which told the universe that she was a full Trader.

She paused at a table five up from theirs and spoke to the hiring crew. A Terran crew as it happened, and it seemed to him that she spoke that language easily, switching seamlessly to Trade when one of those behind the table put a question to her thus.

There seemed some interest on both sides, and, indeed, she did leave a stick with them before taking her leave and moving once more down the row.

She was near enough now that he could see her face–round, and amiable, and pale. Terran herself, then, he thought, with a sharp stab of regret. That might not be so well. The two Terrans they had spoken to on the day had been capable enough in their own language, which he was in the process of Learning, himself, but utterly at a loss in Liaden, and neither proficient in hand-talk.

She passed on, and raised her eyes to look past those who were done for the day, and read the sign on their table.

Her eyes were the color of the Tree's leaves, seen through morning mist. They widened somewhat, and he expected her to pass them by.

She surprised him, however, and quickened her pace until she stood before their table.

She bowed the bow of introduction, and straightened to address them, her face smooth and properly Liaden.

"Pilots. I am Karil Danac-Joenz, Trader, lately serving aboard *Argost*. I am interested in learning your requirements. Perhaps we might benefit each other."

Gods, her Liaden was better than his. Fer Gun managed to keep his countenance, though it took him too long to find his voice, and Chi spoke first, in Terran.

"Trader Danac-Joenz, well-met. We offer a new route which will require fine-tuning, a new captain and crew, and an older small trader. Are you up for a challenge?"

The trader grinned, in that moment utterly Terran.

"Pilot, if I weren't a fool for challenge, I wouldn't have become a trader, over all the objections of my family, who wanted a calm life for me."

Chi inclined her head, and spoke next in Trade.

"You are under contract. When will you be at liberty?"

"My contract with *Argost* expires in two months Standard. The captain has a standing arrangement with an affiliated Line, and an appropriate trader has just recently finished out his contract. As matters stand at the moment, I will be set down at Boert'ani Station. That may be adjusted, of course."

"It is possible that our interests may align," Chi said, back into Liaden, but less formal, closer to his own most comfortable dialect. "May we offer a key?"

"I receive your key with pleasure," Karil Danac-Joenz said, her dock-side bearing an odd Terran inflection, but perfectly intelligible to his ear. "May I offer my own key?"

Chi glanced to him, and back to the trader.

"I am Chi yos'Phelium, representing Korval's interests in this set-up period. This–" she half-bowed in his direction–"is Captain Fer Gun pen'Uldra, who will be regular on the route."

Trader Danac-Joenz turned to him and bowed.

"Captain–" the Liaden word.

"Trader," he answered, in his poor Terran. "I am pleased to accept your key."

She put it on the table before him with dispatch–Liaden manners, again. She had handed her key directly to the Terran recruiter, five tables up.

He inclined his head, and on a hunch added the hand-sign for *well-met.*

"I'm pleased to meet you, too," she said her fluid Terran, her fingers answering *well-met*, with just the right emphasis to convey, also, *agreed.*

* * *

The three resumes they had gathered were surely worthy, Chi thought, watching the crowd thin. Since she had the benefit of Petrella's notes, she knew to a whisker precisely *how* worthy. One at least would serve *Comet* well and honorably, though the raising up of a new captain might try her somewhat.

It would do, she thought, if nothing else presented, and the hour for presenting was growing late. They might take another day here at Dameeth–the schedule was that loose–to see if something more promising arrived on the morrow. On the other hand, there was no certainty that tomorrow would produce any more interesting choices.

She felt Fer Gun shift in the chair next to her. The child was about to suggest that they strike their table and retire to the ship, to study what they had gained. Not an unreasonable suggestion, yet something other than the weight of her belly kept her in her own seat, waiting–

There was a stir at the doorway, and a trader, short for a Terran, tall for a Liaden, moved down the line of tables, deliberately, scanning each in turn. She strolled past the two big-ship tables, with a Terran smile and a nod, and paused at the table which represented the Lazarus Line, which had a long-Loop in need of a trader.

That conversation went well, sticks were exchanged, and the trader moved on, past the empty table, and that being dismantled. She raised her head, read their sign, and glanced to Fer Gun.

Her eyes widened; her lips parted slightly.

Well, now; this was interesting.

The trader stepped forward and introduced herself, and Chi drew a careful breath. She recognized the name, from Petrella's notes.

Interesting; nearly an original. Contracted three years to Argost, and has achieved wonders, despite the limits placed upon her. Possibly Korval will want her, after she's tempered a bit more.

Tempering, thought Chi. Surely it would do the trader no harm, if Korval took active part in her tempering?

Fer Gun had lost the use of his tongue, she noted; first contact was hers to make.

She smiled, therefore, wide and Terran.

"Trader Danac-Joenz," she said cheerfully; "well-met."

VII

"Station master assigns us inner ring twelfth quadrant."

"Got it," Fer Gun answered.

Copilot was riding comm, which is how they had worked out the board between them. In addition, she had a good eye for a likely berth, and the in-ring at twelve was about as likely as they could get, coming in to Boert'ani Station.

Their pick-up here was personnel, in particular, Trader Karil Danac-Joenz.

He was still. . .not entirely certain how Karil Danac-Joenz had come to be their first choice for *Comet's* trader. She was young, she was Terran–well, she had been born into the Terran population on a world that supposed itself Liaden, and was therefore what Chi was pleased to call cross-cultured. She was well-spoken in three languages and in hand-talk, was Trader Danac-Joenz. He had *liked* her, but–the last seven months had taught him the value of having an older and more experienced crewmate to draw upon. And thus he had settled upon Trader Losan vey'Norember, experienced, sober, and very able to advise a new and, despite all his best efforts, ever-to-remain-foolish pilot-captain.

Chi, however, had seen benefit in Trader Danac-Joenz's ease in two cultures, and presented as uniquely useful that the trader held both a five-year trade key from TerraTrade *and* wore the garnet of a Liaden trader.

It had been Chi's opinion that a new route wanted youth and flexibility.

"Old heads tend to be hard heads," she said. "A young captain and a young trader grow together into a team, plan routes and expansions between them; get to know each other's minds. Where you'll want older heads, if I may be so bold, Captain Fer Gun, will be on your copilot and your engineer. And if it were up to me, I'd hire general crew with multiple areas of expertise, rather than just muscle, but you'll suit yourself, of course."

He valued Chi's opinion, and so set himself to compare the resumes of both contenders.

And in the records, he saw Chi's point. The elder trader was surely elder, her list of accomplishments, as one might expect, many times longer than that of the younger trader. But the list of her contacts had been static for years, and the rate of gain for new was. . .slow. Very slow, indeed.

Trader Danac-Joenz, on the other hand, *had* to develop markets and contacts precisely because she *was* new. Further, those markets she had developed remained with her, even as she added to her contacts and expanded her areas of expertise.

And that was how Karil Danac-Joanz had come to receive their offer first, and had accepted it on the spot.

It had been, Fer Gun told himself, his decision, based on Chi's recommendations. Chi's experience.

He only hoped it worked out as she had fortold.

He would, Fer Gun thought, sending a glance over to second chair, miss his copilot, her bossy ways and her encyclopedic knowledge of ships, trade routes, goods, and human persons. More, he would miss her humor, and her patience, and her generosity in bed–oh, he had learned much, this trip, and not merely the ship, and the names of those to whom she introduced him as her business partner, and proper business manners. She had said at the start that she would be generous, and she had more than kept her promise.

Boert'ani Station was their next-to-last stop. Take on the trader, that was one thing; take on a small cargo bound for Lytaxin.

Chi had kin at Lytaxin, and she was under some obligation to show them her belly. That weighed on her, as even he could see; weighed on her enough that he had broached the notion of arranging for another ship to take Lytaxin's small cargo, so she might spare herself at least that burden of propriety.

She had smiled, and kissed his cheek, as if they were true kin and not merely contracted.

"But you know, it must be done. *All* the forms must be observed for this child; and if I make any misstep, it must be in the direction of Too High."

That was just *melant'i* games and High House spite, so far as he'd been able to determine, which had made him glad to be so insignificant, and sorry that she must bear with such nonsense, when she must have a care for the babe on his own account. Surely, this had been no good time for her to take up the frustrating hobby of polishing rough pilots, but she had never stinted him.

Navcomp pinged, and he looked to his boards to find that the approach to their berth had arrived from the station master's office.

"Course received," he said quietly, fingers moving; "locked in."

He glanced over to second board.

"End of shift, Pilot?" he asked–a broad hint; "I'll take her in."

"Glutton," Chi said cheerfully. She rose, carefully though without strain, from her chair. They kept ship's gravity a trifle light so that there would *be* no strain; that had been his idea. She had noticed, of course–Chi yos'Phelium noticed *everything*–but beyond a raised eyebrow had made no comment, which he took to mean light grav might remain.

"Tea, Captain?" she asked him. "A board-snack?"

"Both would be welcome," he said. "I thank you."

"Copilot's duty," she said lightly.

That was proper enough. Still, he might have felt a pang, that she was required to perform such small tasks for him, had she not regaled him with tales of her time as a scout, and confessed that this trip to establish him had benefit to her, as well.

"Far better for me to be here, where things are so much more straightforward and sensible, than negotiating the gathers, and the *melant'i* games, and turning the attempted strikes against Kareen, poor child."

Kareen, had not, he thought, cared much for him. Not that she hadn't a full pod of good reasons to dislike him, not least because he was the instrument by which she would be denied what ought to have been her proper place in her clan. Having been the less-than-able among his own kin, he felt a sympathy for Kareen, but possessed nowhere near the address necessary to express such a thing to her.

And, really, they were not *that* much alike, when he thought more deeply upon it. He was a barely-lettered pilot from a clan which was no higher than it should be, his failing a lack of imagination in the matter of extortion.

Kareen, on the other hand, was a brilliant scholar, gifted in the field of social science, valuable to her clan as he had not–would never be. It was merely that she was not a pilot, and so, by Korval's own law, she could not stand delm.

"Well," Chi had said, one evening as they lay together in bed, sated and in a mood to tell over history. "It is a difficulty with charters made so long ago. We ought, perhaps, to modernize ourselves, but we have obligations every bit as ancient, and so we abide."

She had smiled as he recalled it, wistfully, and murmured.

"Perhaps someday there will be no reason for the delm of Korval to be a master-class pilot. But that day will not, I think, dawn within my lifetime."

The child they had made, then, had best *be* a pilot, capable of mastering Jump at the very least, else Clan Korval would undergo a change–a small change, so it would seem on its face. yos'Galan would ascend to the primary Line, and yos'Phelium would fall into the subordinate place.

It was plain to him. . .say it was plain to him *now*, having had his eyes opened somewhat to nuance by close association with the most complicated mind he had yet met–that the possibility of yos'Phelium failing troubled her.

"Those who came before you ought to have seen the clan-house full of pilots," he said to her, which was surely an impertinence, but she had merely given him a wry smile.

"We were more plentiful before we became embroiled in intemperate politics, and three of our delms came mad–two with the notion that yos'Phelium's connection to the old universe made us a blight upon this one, and far better that the Line died out."

"Do you hold with that?" he asked, not believing it of her.

"How can I believe us to be utterly evil?" she answered, whimsical as she was when she did not care to answer a question too closely. "And, you know, it is not the loss of precedence which I care for, but that we will lose our wings. From the very first, we were pilots, and to fail of being pilots, ever again–perhaps it were best that the Line die out."

That had been too melancholy for pillow-talk, and he had set himself to bring her into a happier frame of mind, which he flattered himself he had done.

And he hoped, that for once in his life, he had been apt.

The proximity sensor beeped at him, then, and he looked to his screens, fingers already moving across the board, making minute adjustments, dancing with the station, and made a wager with himself that he would dock her tight on the first attempt.

#

He won his wager handsomely, sliding into dock with no slightest bobble. He refused station air, and the list of dockside services. Station would know that they were short-dockers, Chi not having been likely to have omitted that detail in negotiating their space. Still, he supposed they had to ask, on the chance that the PIC was an idiot, or the ship had a surplus of funds. Their bad luck that the pilot had lately graduated from idiot to half-wit, and ship's funds were adequate for the necessities, without running to luxury.

Details settled, he opened the port directory, meaning to place a call to cor'Wellin Warehousing, and arrange delivery of the cargo bound for Lytaxin.

Before he could open an outgoing line, though, the comm lit green–call incoming.

He touched the switch.

"*Comet.*"

"Good spin, *Comet*," said a light, cheerful voice, speaking Liaden in the mode between comrades, "this is Karil Danac-Joenz. Do I speak with Pilot pen'Uldra?"

"Trader, you do," he said, meeting her in comrade. "I hope you are well."

"Well, but bored–you cannot imagine how much!" she told him. "The market here is dismal and the trade floors–as Boert'ani Station acts as my host, I will say only that the trade floors are bland in the extreme. There. We need never speak of it again."

His lips twitched.

"Will you come aboard, then? I warn you that we are also bland, sitting at dock as we do."

"But that is an affliction which will soon be remedied, will it not?" she said, and before he could answer, swept on, "Yes, Pilot, I would very much like to come aboard. May I? Soon?"

"Yes," he said. "What is your direction? I have a delivery to arrange, but then I will come for you. Have you much luggage?"

There was a small pause, as if he had surprised the trader.

"Pilot, thank you. I am at the Spinside Hyatt, and can be at your hatch within the hour. As to luggage, I assure you that I require no assistance."

He hesitated, but Boert'ani was rated safe, after all, and surely a trader must be dock-wise.

"Come, then, and welcome," he told her. "We will expect you."

"Excellent! Until soon."

"Until soon," he answered, but the light had already gone out.

Well, then. On to the next task. He located cor'Wellin in the port directory and placed his call.

"This is Fer Gun pen'Uldra," he told the man who answered; "small trader *Comet*. I wish to arrange delivery of our cargo, hold number CW9844."

The warehouseman's face changed. Perhaps it was dismay. He held his hands up to the screen.

"My apologies, Pilot, but you must come to us. Your cargo has been damaged. You will want to inspect it before taking delivery."

"Damaged? What kind of damage?"

The man licked his lips.

"I cannot say, Pilot. It will be best for you to come yourself, perform an inspection and file a damage report, if you deem it necessary."

Fer Gun glared at the warehouseman. The warehouseman simply stared back at him.

"I will be there within the hour," he said curtly, and cut the connection.

He had hoped to let Chi sleep her fill; and now he would have to wake her for board-duty–another irritation.

Well, it couldn't be helped.

He rose, and crossed the bridge to the main hall –

A bell rang.

Fer Gun frowned–then his face cleared. Trader Danac-Joenz had arrived. Perhaps he could let Chi sleep after all.

He turned left, down the access hall, glanced at the screen, and verified that the tall woman with the amiable face, and her pretty brown hair braided down her back today was, indeed, Karil Danac-Joenz–and cycled the hatch.

#

Chi was in the co-pilot's chair when they came onto the bridge, having stopped on the way from the hatch to stow the trader's meager luggage in her quarters.

Fer Gun swallowed a curse.

"Pilot," Chi said agreeably. "Hello, Trader; well-met."

"Pilot." Trader Danac-Joenz bowed. "It's good to be aboard."

"It's good to have you," Chi assured her, then turned a sapient eye to him.

"What's amiss, Fer Gun?"

He sighed.

"The warehouse lets me know that the cargo for Lytaxin is damaged. They won't deliver until I've gone to the warehouse, inspected the damage and filled out some paperwork. I had hoped to let you rest. In fact, why not rest again? The trader will stand comm."

He saw Chi look aside, and followed her gaze. Karil Danac-Joenz was frowning slightly.

"Yes?" Chi murmured. "Do not hesitate to share your thoughts, Trader. You will find it a plain-spoken ship."

A subtle grin briefly illuminated the trader's face before she turned to Fer Gun.

"Unless Pilot yos'Phelium's need is dire, I think the ship is better served if I go with you to the warehouse," she said. "I am something of an expert on cargo, and on the sorts of damage cargo might reasonably receive."

She paused, not quite a hesitation, and bowed slightly.

"I am also an expert on paperwork having to do with cargo." She gave him a whimsical look. "My master insisted that I learn it all, no matter how tedious, and well it was that he did–the garnet exams are nearly all about paperwork."

It was his decision. Chi could have said, "That would be the best use of resources, Pilot." She *didn't* say it, but he heard it inside his head, just as clearly as if she had. And, yes, he told himself grumpily, it was the best use of available resources.

"Well, then," he said, bowing lightly; "are you ready now, Trader?"

She returned the bow.

"Yes, let us go now. It's a lovely day for a walk."

#

"I am here," Fer Gun told the clerk behind the counter, "to inspect cargo that was damaged. Lot Number CW9844, on hold for *Comet*."

She glanced down, presumably at a screen set below the counter, and looked up again, face stiff.

"Lot CW9844 is being held in the inspection bay. Down this hall, Pilots, to the end. There is a door."

"We will require the presence of a warehouse representative," Trader Danac-Joenz said. "We were told there would be paperwork."

The clerk took a breath.

"Someone will be waiting for you in the inspection bay."

There was a momentary hesitation, as if the trader had weighed this answer and found it wanting. Then, she inclined her head, and turned to him.

"After you, Pilot."

#

The hall was short, and oddly unpeopled. Fer Gun hesitated, and glanced at his trader.

"Do you have a weapon?"

She met his eyes.

"Will I need one?"

"I don't know," he admitted, and moved a hand, fingers flickering in the sign for *bad feeling*. "You won't wait in the hall, I suppose."

She laughed.

"Already, we are beginning to know each other! No, Pilot; I will not wait in the hall, but I will cover your off-side."

Well, that was fair enough, he owned; and, by the look of her, it was the trader's best offer.

"To my right, then," he said, and lengthened his stride, so he was first through the door.

The bay was bright-lit, which he hadn't expected; and there was the pallet, in the center of the light, looking remarkably unscathed. He cleared the door for his back-up–six strides beyond the door–and stopped, looking to the right of the cargo, where the light had thrown shadows.

"Jai Kob," he said, finding the first cousin easy enough, leaning against a pod-lift, just at the edge of the shadow.

A longer look brought him the second, deeper in the dimness, crouching on his heels.

"Vin Dyr," he added, and over his shoulder–"My cousins."

"Is that the contract-wife?" Jai Kob asked, strolling forward, his hands tucked comfortably into his belt. He gave the trader an appraising glance, and looked back to Fer Gun, frowning.

"Withholding yourself, Gunny? Or just inept?"

"I was told," Fer Gun said, watching out of the side of his eye as Vin Dyr straightened to his feet. "That my cargo was damaged, and required an inspection, with a paper filed. Working for the warehouse, cousin?"

Jai Kob laughed, and Vin Dyr drifted closer to the light. Fer Gun felt the trader's attention shift in that direction.

"The cargo's well-enough, so far as my inspection goes," Jai Kob said. "Given the terms of the contract you're under, we thought it best to meet you in private. *Is* that the contract-wife?"

"No," said Trader Danac-Joenz.

"Good," Jai Kob said. "That's good."

He stepped closer, his hands slipping out of his belt. There was a packet in his off-hand, which he lifted slightly to show Fer Gun.

"The damage call was only a prank, Gunny–just a joke between kin. But it's true enough that you've papers to sign."

Fer Gun felt his stomach clench. Papers. Often enough, he'd had papers to sign, since the day he came halfling; his grandfather gone, and what care he had coming from his clever older cousins.

The very same older cousins who had given him papers to sign at Solcintra Port, scheming to strip his wings away, and likely long-ago murdered in the Low Port, if Chi yos'Phelium's iron whim hadn't settled on him.

"What papers?" he asked Jai Kob. "Agreeing to an extra fee for the release of the pod?"

Jai Kob looked hurt, which meant nothing. Jai Kob could assume any expression or attitude the moment wanted.

"Are we pod-pirates, Gunny?" he asked and swept on before Fer Gun could answer, which was just as well. "No, we've only this paper here that needs your signature. You remember the quarterlies. Well, it's past time for the next."

He remembered the quarterlies, so he did. The very first one signed at his cousins' direction barely three days after his grandfather's death. He hadn't read that one. Jai Kob had assured him there was no need; Jai Kob had read it, after all, and had found everything in order.

"What's that about the marriage contract?" he asked, then.

"Didn't they tell you, Gunny? Korval was paying Telrune a handsome sum for your...abilities, but just the smallest taste up-front, and all the rest on completion, contingent on no kin contacting you during the marriage."

"So you've just breached the terms," Fer Gun pointed out. "Telrune will like that you've snatched cantra out of his fingers."

"The little cousin's gotten sharp," Vin Dyr said dryly, stepping fully into the light.

Jai Kob shook his head.

"Who's to know it, unless you tattle, and then Telrune will know right enough who to blame. But, here, Gunny, I can see you're in no mood to play. Just sign the paper, we'll be off, and you can take delivery of your cargo."

Fer Gun took a deep breath, teetering on the edge of choice. Sign the paper and Jai Kob released the cargo in good order. Refuse to sign the paper, and the cargo would not survive the next hour, no matter how good his cousin's humor appeared.

To allow Korval's cargo to be destroyed because he had grown squeamish about his cousins. Was that even a choice?

It occurred to him then that there was a third choice.

"Trader Danac-Joenz," he heard himself say calmly; "of your kindness."

"Certainly, Captain."

She stepped forward and held out her hand for the packet.

Jai Kob took a step back, glaring.

"What's this, Gunny?"

"This is the ship's trader," Fer Gun said. "I brought her to deal with the paperwork for the damaged cargo."

"This is between cousins," Jai Kob protested. "It's not for anyone to look at and blab around the docksides."

"Sir." Trader Danac-Joenz sounded halfway between angry and amused. "I am, in fact, *Comet's* trader. I assure you–I know how to treat confidential business. If you would care to step up the hall to the office, I will call up my references for you."

Jai Kob stared, frozen in place. Vin Dyr shifted, boots grating on the floor as he adjusted his balance, his hand moving toward the place where he kept his hideaway. Fer Gun stepped to the side, and waved the trader forward, putting her and Jai Kob into the same frame.

It was still a risk, Vin Dyr being more than a fair shot, but he wouldn't take the snap-shot now, just to see what would happen, not with Jai Kob so near.

At least, Fer Gun hoped so.

"The trader will review the paperwork," he said; "to be certain that everything is in order. Surely, cousin, you don't want to risk Tel-rune's anger on a faulty instrument."

"*Faulty instrument*," Vin Dyr repeated, not quite under his breath. "The child has airs."

Fer Gun ignored him.

"Will you be able to work here, Trader? Or will the warehouse office be better?"

"This is perfectly adequate," she assured him. "This light is particularly good. Now, if the gentleman will relinquish the packet. . .?"

For a moment, Fer Gun thought that Jai Kob would do no such thing. It was possible that Jai Kob thought so, too.

Then, he took one step forward–and placed the packet into the trader's outstretched hand.

"Thank you," she said with complete composure.

And broke the seal.

#

"The third paragraph references the terms of a previous contract, dated some dozen Standards back," Trader Danac-Joenz murmured, "which would appear to be the foundation for the rest of this currently proposed document."

She looked up from the papers and gave Fer Gun a bright, candid glance.

"You have that contract among your records, of course, Captain. Will it be available to the ship's system?"

Fer Gun felt his stomach clench, as in the back of his mind, he heard Lady yo'Lanna scolding him: *Read the contract; understand the contract; keep a copy of the contract for future consultation.*

"My cousins have been in the habit of keeping my paperwork for me," he told the trader, and waited for the scorn to fill her eyes.

Instead, her eyes narrowed, and if there was any emotion on her face, he would have said it was anger.

"I see. Naturally, you would have been very young when the foundation document was made, and it would have been natural for elder kin to hold the files. They ought, of course, to have transferred the records to you when you came of age, but such things often slip the mind.

"Happily, we can regularize the situation now."

She turned to Jai Kob.

"If you will kindly bring forth those records, sir, I may continue my work. Thus far, the contract you offer appears. . .promising. But we must, as I am certain you understand, have the foundation document. Indeed, it ought to have been appended to this paper–but again, it is so very easy for such details to slip the mind."

Boot soles grated against a gritty floor.

Fer Gun turned sharply toward Vin Dyr, his hand dropping to the gun on his belt.

His cousin twitched–and raised both hands, showing them empty.

"The foundation document," Jai Kob was saying in the quick, light voice he used when he was lying. "Certainly, Trader; how foolish of me to have forgotten! There is, in fact, a copy in the ship's files. Unfortunately, with Fer Gun under contract, we have no third to leave on-board while Vin Dyr and I attend business. It will require only an hour to go to the ship and bring back the complete files for you to peruse. If you would care to wait here? Or–of course! The trade bar. We will meet you there, in an hour, if that will suffice you?"

Fer Gun kept his warning behind his teeth. Korval's cargo, he reminded himself; that was the important thing here: To recover the cargo intact.

"Certainly," Trader Danac-Joenz said cordially. "An hour, in the Trade Bar. We will be much more comfortable there, and will have access to the library, should there be need."

"Excellent," Jai Kob said. He extended a hand to the trader, for the contract. She merely looked at him.

"I will keep this, of your kindness," she said, "and continue my review. I know that your time is valuable."

"Just so," said Jai Kob, and bowed.

"Trader," he said. "Gunny." He glanced aside.

"Come along, cousin," he said to Vin Dyr, who needed no such urging. Walking briskly, they were through the door–and gone.

"What are the odds," Trader Danac-Joenz said, lightly, her eyes on the door, "that they will come back in an hour, with or without those documents?"

"No odds, Trader. Next we hear, they'll be casting off without having filed with the station master."

She nodded, reached to her belt, and pulled out a portcomm.

"Ship's name?" she murmured, thumbing the call button.

"*Lady Graz*."

"Thank you." She tipped her head.

"Pilot yos'Phelium, this is Karil Danac-Joenz. We have a situation," she said crisply. "Can you–or Korval–hold the ship *Lady Graz* at dock?"

VII

Chi sat in the co-pilot's chair. She had the surveillance camera feeding screen three, though she expected no trouble on their own dock. Frowning, she examined that thought.

No, she decided, the trouble, whatever shape it took, would be with the cargo. Well that Fer Gun hadn't gone alone. Well–well, indeed–that Karil Danac-Joenz was far removed from being a fool. She was encouraged on that front, very much so.

She glanced at the clock. An hour gone, and no word from either. That could be good news. Or bad news. Or no news at all.

"You're as jumpy as a cat with one kitten," she growled at herself–and snapped forward when the comm pinged.

"*Comet*," she snapped, and frowned slightly at Karil Danac-Joenz' voice.

"Not even Korval holds ships at a whim," she said. "We need a reason that will compel the station master."

"It will have to be piracy, Pilot. Pilot pen'Uldra's cousins met us at the warehouse, wishing him to sign a document. *Very much* wishing for him to sign a document, and desperate enough for it that they were holding our cargo ransom.

"My reading of this document leads me to believe that they have been cheating Pilot pen'Uldra of the profits of his birth-right since before he came of age. The present scheme is to transfer the ship wholly to them, and to strip him of all his assets."

Chi closed her eyes and counted to one hundred forty-four. How one did *long* to speak, personally and alone, with the cousins.

"Do you have the document?" Chi asked, keeping her voice calm.

"I have the new document," the trader said. "The case would be stronger, with the entire series in hand." She paused. "Pilot pen'Uldra's cousins have said that they are going back to their ship to retrieve those, and will meet us at the trade bar inside of an hour."

Chi gave a sharp laugh.

"Yes, exactly. You see why it must be piracy?"

"I do, indeed. Where are you and Fer Gun now?"

"At the warehouse."

"Come home," Chi said. "Leave the damned cargo. Until we have a chance to order a comprehensive scan, it is compromised, and it is not coming anywhere near this ship."

"Yes, pilot. Agreed."

"Good. I'll call the station master, and file our complaint."

* * *

"Thank you, Pilot; we're on our way."

The trader thumbed off the unit, and looked at Fer Gun.

"Your co-pilot requests you return to the ship."

"The cargo?"

"We're to treat it as compromised and a danger to the ship."

He almost smiled at that. Trust Chi yos'Phelium to protect the ship.

"Right," he said, and jerked his head toward the door. "Let's go."

Together they exited the inspection bay.

He stopped at the office to let the clerk know that the cargo was to remain isolated until it had been thoroughly inspected by a third party. She pushed him to leave a deposit for the space, he said curtly that he would do so when the inspection was complete, and in the meantime, he expected the bay to placed under seal.

Possibly, he was too rough. Her face paled somewhat and she lowered her eyes.

"Of course, Pilot."

They were well away from the warehouse when the trader's comm pinged.

"Yes," she said, putting the unit to her ear. She listened, and nodded, Terran-wise.

"Thank you. Yes, we'll go at once."

The comm vanished, and the trader turned to him.

"*Lady Graz* has been locked down, pending a formal filing of piracy."

He looked at her.

"That means. . .?"

"It means," she said, "that you must go to the station master's office and sign some paperwork."

He stiffened, and caught his breath when he felt her hand on his.

"We'll both go, of course, and read the papers together."

Fer Gun managed a smile.

"Of course," he said. "My thanks, Trader."

"If we're going to be working together, I think I ought to be Karil," she said, still keeping a hold on his hand, as she turned them back to the station master's office.

"In that wise, I will be Fer Gun," he answered, and traded her, smile for smile.

VIII

Well, and it came to light, once all of the documents were found and accessed, that the first paper he had signed for Jai Kob, giving him free use of the ship *Lady Graz*, which had been left to Fer Gun by his grandfather–that paper had not been regular, at all, since Fer Gun had been too young to sign such a thing.

The second paper gave Jai Kob access to the accounts Grandfather had left to Fer Gun, himself, and also immortalized Fer Gun's agreement to pay for any repairs and upgrades required to *Lady Graz* from his own funds.

That, too, was irregular, having been presented to the still-grieving Fer Gun barely two days after the paper which had stolen away his ship.

At the last, it was a matter for *Qe'andra* dea'Gauss to sort out, which was done. Jai Kob and Vin Dyr had been fined, blacklisted, stripped of all licenses, and placed on an ore boat as working crew, their wages limited to berth and meals. Eventually, they would arrive home, and Telrune would deal with them. . .not kindly, as Fer Gun saw it. They had lost the ship, the money, Telrune's portion of the marriage settlement, and exposed themselves to discovery and punishment. He could not predict what further penalty the delm might place upon his cousins, but he doubted it would be pleasant.

In the meanwhile, there was work to be done–he had two ships now, though *Lady* was in need of upgrading, as well as new licenses and registrations. A deal was closed with Korval's Chonselta Yard for the refurbs, which would take up the year of *Comet's* first real run; and another with *Qe'andra* dea'Gauss for the applications and the purges and the clear new record.

He'd taken crew on for *Comet*; and Karil had emerged from several hours closeted with Chi's sister, the master trader, with an amended route, a goods list, and a thick notebook full of contacts.

There remained one more duty to perform, as per the contract, and he was there at the early hour of the morning Chi's son had chosen for his entrance into the world. He stood witness as the child was born, and examined, and pronounced fit. And he remained there when the room was cleared of Healer and medic and the Council's eyes. At her invitation, he sat on the edge of the bed, covering her hand with his, and smiled at the boy with his sharp black eyes, and his black hair, already rumpled and unruly.

"When do you lift?" she asked him.

"Tomorrow morning," he answered. "We can file an amendment, if you have need of me."

She smiled at that.

"I see no reason for such desperate measures as that," she murmured, still half-drowsy with whatever the Healer had done.

"Then, tomorrow morning, we're away; and returning to Liad in a year, to outfit the *Lady* and see her crewed."

"Come and see me, Pilot, when you're back again," she said, and he squeezed her hand lightly.

"I must, after all; you'll want an accounting of the ship's business."

"Which you may and shall file with dea'Gauss," she said with a faint smile. "Come to me anyway."

"I will," he promised.

She closed her eyes, then. The boy–Daav yos'Phelium–stared at him for another minute from knowing dark eyes, before he, too, slipped away into sleep.

EPILOG

Daav and Er Thom were having a game of tag back and forth across the Tree Court. At least Chi supposed it to be tag, though she conceded the possibility that it was some other game of their own devising, the rules of which she was not meant to know.

In any case, it involved a great deal of running around, and shouting, and dodging behind bushes in order to lay in wait, and leap out at one's brother, whereupon there was laughter on both sides, and a bound once more into action.

There had also been what she allowed to be only the most necessary amount of rolling about in the grass, and at least one unfortunate encounter with the gloan roses, which had taken, so she believed, no permanent damage. The scratches, she had declared minor, and the game was therefore rejoined.

She. . .was supposed to be reading the agenda and briefing documents for the next meeting of the Council of Clans. Indeed, the material lay on the bench beside her, though she had not even glanced at them, finding the play of her sons–of her son and Petrella's–to be far more compelling.

They made a striking pair, grass-stained and perspiring as they were. The eldest, Er Thom, Petrella's lad, was already a beauty, with gilt hair and violet eyes surrounded by dark gold lashes. He looked, in fact, quite a lot like Petrella, and so very much like his foster-mother, Chi.

By contrast, Daav was lean and vulpine, a changeling, with his dark hair, dark eyes, and marked brows. It was well that she had made her pregnancy and his birth a matter of very public record, indeed. Looking at him, even if he could be persuaded for five minutes to stand still, never mind remaining clean, unrumpled, and with his hair combed–even then, he could scarce be taken for one of Korval, never mind the delm-to-be.

Well, and it was too soon, yet, to know if Daav would in fact be delm. If not, the Ring would fall to Er Thom. And however it went, Korval would have at his side his brother, who had been given exactly the same education, shared the same history, and stood always as a valuable and beloved ally.

"Catch me!" Daav cried, and bolted for the Tree, rounding the enormous trunk with nary a stumble, despite the plentiful surface roots waiting to catch the feet of the unwary.

Er Thom flew after him, every bit as nimble, and vanished on the far side of the Tree.

She felt it then–say it was a small flutter in the air, or a puff of pleasure at seeing an old friend. She turned her head so that she could see the path, and here he came, tall, and lean, and. . .somewhat less wolfish when first she had seen him.

The leather jacket hugged shoulders that had filled out; shoulders that wore the easy weights of success and satisfaction. The dark hair was tidy, if still over-long; the face fuller at cheek and jaw.

He raised a hand as he left the path. She smiled and moved the unread papers beneath the bench.

"Fer Gun," she said. "Well-met."

"Well-met," he answered and settled next to her with the ease of an old friend. "We came in early and I thought I'd call before we're swamped tomorrow with business."

"Is Karil with you?" she asked, already knowing that she was not.

"Not today, though she hopes to see you before we lift again," he said, and turned his head sharply at the whoop from behind the Tree and the sudden appearance of two small bodies, running flat out toward the rose bank again.

"They're in fine fettle," Fer Gun said, and gave her a sideways glance. "I do regret that mode, you know. There was no reason he should look like me when he had you as a model."

"Well, there is something to be said for contrariness," she said comfortably. "It's a family trait, after all."

His wide mouth softened into a smile, and he leaned back as Daav flung his arms out, shouted, "Zooooom!" and banked hard, only brushing the flowers, and flew back toward the tree, trailing rose petals.

"Here's a bit of news you'll enjoy," Fer Gun said. "We were approached by Telrune regarding an accounting owed the clan."

"Were you? How did that go?"

He moved his shoulders.

"Karil sent a copy of our incorporation as a Family, and the contact information for our *qe'andra*."

Another slight shrug.

"We received in return a rather curt letter stating that it would have been good form, had I contacted Telrune to *formally sever* my connection with the clan. I'm properly put into my place."

Chi laughed.

"I see that you are. And the children?"

"Telrune has no claim on our children," Fer Gun said sternly. His voice softened as he added, "If they tried to lay such a claim, they would have to go through Karil."

"Daunting, for bolder hearts than Telrune, if I may be forgiven for speaking so of your clan."

"Not my clan, haven't you been listening? We're Family Uldra-Joenz, incorporated on Fetzer's World."

"Fer Gun!" a young voice yelled, and here came Daav pelting across the grass, Er Thom a fleet shadow at his side.

Fer Gun came to his feet in a rush, swooping the lean body up, spinning as he held the boy over his head.

Daav shouted with laughter, and collapsed flat on his back in the grass when he was let down so Er Thom could have his turn.

"Well, my sons," said Chi, when the merriment had somewhat abated. "I believe it is time the two of you bowed to the necessity of baths, and study. You may join me for Prime on the east patio, unless you have other obligations."

"We have no other obligations," Er Thom said gravely. "Thank you, Mother."

"Will Fer Gun stay for Prime?" Daav wanted to know.

"Not today," Fer Gun answered. "Maybe your mother won't be too busy to have me and my lady back, sometime before we're set to lift again."

"We will arrange a time," Chi said, standing, and waving the boys toward the path. "Make your bows, now."

They did, very prettily, if briefly, before breaking to race for the path.

"Bathe!" Chi called after them, and bent to retrieve her paperwork.

"I don't know," Fer Gun said, as they followed the boys at a more sedate pace; "if I ever properly thanked you for all of the good things you brought into my life. In fact, you *saved* my life." He paused, and took a breath, before meeting her eyes.

"I don't know that there is any *proper* thanks for such gifts. Notice that I say gifts, because there is no hope I can bring us into Balance."

There came a shriek of laughter from the path ahead, and he raised his eyebrows.

Chi smiled.

"We are perfectly in Balance, my friend," tucking her hand into his arm and increasing their leisurely pace somewhat.

"Let us speak no more about it."

–end–

PINBEAM BOOKS

For a complete catalog of all eChapbooks available through Pinbeam Books, please see www.pinbeambooks.com[1]

Chapbooks are added on an irregular basis, so do check back often.

1. http://www.pinbeambooks.com/

About This Book

It is a fact little known that Lee and Miller do not write every story that occurs to them. In order to be written, stories must have staying power. They must, in a word, put themselves forward and continue to do so until one or the other–or both–of us throw up our hands in surrender and say, "All right–*all right*! If we write you will you leave us in peace?"

We first talked about a writing a story that was kinda, sorta like "Due Diligence," oh. . .back in, oh, 2008, when we were getting *Fledgling* ready to submit to Baen. We jotted it down as a possible, but. . .it just didn't put itself forward, and in the way of such things, we forgot about it.

It, however, did not forget about us.

Oh, no. It sat back, and bided its time, and grew deeper and wider and more complex, until, suddenly, at the most inconvenient time possible–as we were gearing up to write the last book in a five book arc–it hurled itself across the highway of creative thought, completely blocking both lanes, and yelled:

"WRITE ME NOW!"

Now, we know what you're going to say. You're going to say, "I'm not seeing an *or-else* here. It's a story–no, wait; it's *not even* a story; it's *an idea* for a story! It's *nothing* until you guys write it; and it's *got* nothing."

And that's where you'd be wrong.

The one thing that this story–this *proto-story* can do in order to be certain that its demands are met?

Is to just lie there in the middle of the highway of creative thought, and. . .

. . .*be in the way.*

Story-stuff is sticky.

You can't go through it without getting it all over yourself.

Story-stuff is infinitely expandable.

You can't go around it.

You *can* move it, but the way you move story-stuff?

Is to write it.

. . .so that's what we did–and here you have it.

We hope you enjoyed reading the story as much as we, eventually, enjoyed writing it.

Sharon Lee and Steve Miller

Cat Farm and Confusion Factory

Winslow, Maine

July 11, 2017

ABOUT THE AUTHORS

Maine-based writers **Sharon Lee and Steve Miller** teamed up in the late 1980s to bring the world the story of Kinzel, an inept wizard with a love of cats, a thirst for justice, and a staff of true power. Since then, the husband-and-wife have written dozens of short stories and twenty plus novels, most set in their star-spanning, nationally-best-selling, Liaden Universe®.

Before settling down to the serene and stable life of a science fiction and fantasy writer, Steve was a traveling poet, a rock-band reviewer, reporter, and editor of a string of community newspapers.

Sharon, less adventurous, has been an advertising copywriter, copy editor on night-side news at a small city newspaper, reporter, photographer, and book reviewer.

Both credit their newspaper experiences with teaching them the finer points of collaboration.

Steve and Sharon are jointly the recipients of the **E. E. "Doc" Smith Memorial Award for Imaginative Fiction** (the *Skylark*), one of the oldest awards in science fiction. In addition, their work has won the much-coveted **Prism Award** (*Mouse and Dragon* and *Local Custom*), as well as the **Hal Clement Award for Best Young Adult Science Fiction** (*Balance of Trade*).

Sharon and Steve passionately believe that reading fiction ought to be fun, and that stories are entertainment. Steve and Sharon maintain a web presence at http://korval.com/

NOVELS BY SHARON LEE AND STEVE MILLER

The Liaden Universe®

Fledgling

Saltation

Mouse and Dragon

Ghost Ship

Dragon Ship

Necessity's Child

Trade Secret

Dragon in Exile

Alliance of Equals

The Gathering Edge

Neogenesis

Omnibus Editions

The Dragon Variation

The Agent Gambit

Korval's Game

The Crystal Variation

Story Collections

A Liaden Universe Constellation: Volume 1

A Liaden Universe Constellation: Volume 2
A Liaden Universe Constellation: Volume 3

The Fey Duology

Duainfey
Longeye

Gem ser'Edreth

The Tomorrow Log

by Sharon Lee

Carousel Tides
Carousel Sun
Carousel Seas

THANK YOU

Thank you for your support of our work.

Sharon Lee and Steve Miller

Made in the USA
San Bernardino, CA
18 January 2018